The Doll Girl

Also by Abigail Davies
(writing as A. E. Richards)

Blackened Cottage
Loch Boy
Diary of a Born Survivor
War of Men
Girl Disturbed

The Doll Girl

ABIGAIL DAVIES

First published 2019

Copyright © Abigail Davies

The author asserts her moral right under the Copyright, Designs and Patents Act, 1988, to be identified as the author of this work.

For my daughter, Heidi

Chapter One

Mother had painted my face every morning for as long as I could remember and today was no exception. But today was different in one way. It was my thirteenth birthday. Today I was another year older. Today I couldn't ignore the fact that dolls lived short lives. This fact clung to me like the plague, oozing and pulsating inside my mind, alive as I was soon to be dead. And beside this terrible fact hovered my big question. A question that made my tummy screw itself up into a hard knot.

If Mother sensed my mood, she did not show it. We sat at the dining room table and Mother placed her make up bag on her lap. She unzipped the shiny red purse, humming softly. I wrinkled my nose. The room smelt of urine from the dead roses in the centre of the table. They had died a week ago, but Mother seemed not to notice.

The first part of me that Mother painted was my forehead. With her tongue pinched between her small, yellow teeth, she smoothed white powder over my skin, working up and along my hairline, down and around my eyebrows then down the bridge of my nose and around my nostrils. She smoothed powder onto each cheek and my upper lip, finishing with my chin and jaw. Eyebrows were next. With a black pencil she coloured in the fair hairs above my eyes. When the pencil was due for sharpening the lead scratched, but Mother grew angry if I complained or moved, so I counted the freckles on her face to distract myself. I was up to twenty when she moved on to my eyes.

"So big and blue," she murmured as she often did when she reached this part.

Her warm breath touched my nose and I smelt coffee and buttered toast. I looked at her small, brown eyes, tried to focus on them, focus on anything except for the fact that I was another year older. I thought about how unalike our eyes were. I didn't have freckles, but I did have blonde hair like Mother, whose hair bobbed around her chin. Mine reached my knees. It was ratty at the ends because Mother never cut it. She said she would trim the ends when it reached my ankles. She loved my long yellow hair. Always complained that hers would not grow past her shoulders. Sometimes when she walked past me she ran her fingers down my hair, admiring its glossy feel.

My question trembled on my tongue, but I pushed the words away. Mother didn't like me to talk when she painted me and I had to get the timing absolutely right. For months I had been building up to asking this question. For months I had tested the words on my reflection, watched my eyes widen with anticipation and fear and something else I couldn't name.

Mother patted and smoothed blue powder onto my eyelids, careful to be gentle, then blew the excess away and picked up the mascara wand. When I was little I'd feared this part, but I was used to it now. I kept my eyes open and looked down at the fuzzy tip of my nose, making myself go cross-eyed. A headache started like it always did, but I didn't complain.

I held my breath and sat extra still when Mother curled my

eyelashes, remembering the time five years ago when an itch had made me move and Mother had ripped out a clump of lashes. The pain had been so intense that I hadn't been able to hold in the tears that had rolled down my cheeks and ruined Mother's careful work. I had been sent to my room for the rest of the day and Mother had not spoken to me for three days.

I pushed out my lips keeping them open a slither while Mother lined my mouth with a scarlet pencil and filled in each lip with scarlet lipstick. She slipped a folded tissue between my lips and I closed my mouth on it and silently counted to three. I opened my mouth and Mother withdrew the tissue and dropped it in the wicker bin beside her chair.

Her eyes scanned my face. I waited, breath held, hoping she would not wipe it off and start again. A moment passed. She gave a nod and smiled.

"You're such a beautiful little doll, Mirabelle," she said picking up the hairbrush.

She moved to stand behind me and began to brush my hair with long, slow strokes. This was my favourite part. My shoulders dropped an inch and I concentrated on the wonderful sensation of bristles lightly scraping my scalp, but I could not relax. My question hovered at the front of my mind, on the tip of my tongue, in the jolting beat of my heart.

"Mother?" I said.

"Yes, Mirabelle?"

I hesitated. A hot, dizzy feeling swept across my face. Mother's rhythmic brushing continued, falling in time with every other click of the huge grandfather clock. The heavy navy curtains were pulled shut over the wooden boards that were nailed over the windows, the room a pit of gloom. Not a shred of natural light penetrated the gloom though a little light came from a lamp in the corner. The roses reeked. Roses needed light and air to grow. It was no wonder they were dead.

I swallowed and licked my lips. "Mother, I've been thinking and, well, as it's my thirteenth birthday, I was wondering if, maybe, at dusk, just before dark, I could go out into the back garden - just for a few minutes or so. Surely that wouldn't be too -"

Mother's hand froze halfway down my back. My head throbbed. For a terrifying second I thought she was going to hit me with the hard plastic side of the hairbrush. I waited, unable to breathe, my eyes fixed on the curtains. Tension made my back rigid.

"No," she said quietly.

Her brushing resumed but this time the brush did not lightly scrape my scalp; bristles dug in so forcefully that they scraped through the surface of my skin. I winced and tried to breathe deeply, choking back tears of frustration, disappointment, gritting my teeth with anger - angry at myself for asking when I knew what the answer would be – frustrated with Mother for not even considering what I believed to be a great idea, and all the while trembling with fear.

"How many times do I have to tell you?" she hissed, "It's for your own safety."

She dragged the brush over my grazed scalp a second time.

"I know. I'm so sorry, Mother," I whispered quickly, dropping my head.

She placed the brush on the table and walked around to face me. Her eyes were sad as she crouched down in front of my knees and gently pushed my hair behind my ears.

"You know that I love you - that all I want is to protect you, don't you little doll?"

I nodded and looked at her glistening eyes. She sighed and stood up. Her eyes glinted, the wetness gone in an instant. "I have a special surprise planned for your birthday."

I tried to smile up at her and blinked back tears. "Gosh. Thank you, Mother!"

"That's alright. You're to study Mathematics this morning. Off you go. I'll be in to check your answers in one hour."

In my bedroom, I studied hard. Harder than ever. I wanted to show Mother I was sorry for asking my question. I wanted to impress her with my speed, show her how many questions I could answer in an hour. She'd stopped teaching me last year when she said I'd reached a good level, saying that knowing more than that was useless anyway, especially as dolls lived short lives.

A shudder rocked my body. Thoughts of dying returned, leaking into my mind like bloody puddles. Mother never said when I would die, just that dolls like me were only perfect and healthy when they were young. But how young was young? My hand froze above the textbook. I pushed myself up from the desk and wandered to the mirror.

I didn't look like I was dying. In my beautiful, scarlet dress embroidered with its intricate green and yellow flowers, and with my face painted with such precision and care - my hair as glossy as satin in the weak lamplight - I looked healthy. I sort of glowed. Twinkled. Twinkled like stars I'd never seen, and would never see.

Tears prickled my eyes. I held them back and took a step closer to the mirror. I stared into my own eyes until my vision blurred black. *Mother loves me*, I told myself. My fingers went to my hair, my soft, shiny hair that Mother brushed so tenderly every morning and every night. I touched the sore grazes on my scalp.

She had not drawn blood. Mother never drew blood. *That would destroy my flawlessness*, I thought, surprised by the bitter edge to the words. "Mother loves me," I said into the silence, to my reflection, to the boarded window, to the gloom that forever surrounded me.

A sound outside my room made me dash back to the desk.

"Mirabelle?"

"Yes, Mother?"

"Why weren't you sitting at your desk?"

She moved to stand behind me, placing her hands on my shoulders. Her hands were cold. She was a whole head taller than me, her body long and thin. I craned my neck to peer up at her. She tilted her head to the side and frowned.

"I was admiring my dress in the mirror," I said quickly, feeling a stab of guilt at the lie.

She held my gaze until I looked away. Picking up a red pen from the desk, she bent over me and marked my work.

"One hundred percent, like always. Good doll," she said, patting my shoulder. She placed an apple on my desk, "I'm going out. As it's your birthday, you may read for the rest of the day in here or in the living room, whichever you would prefer."

I gasped and stood up. "Oh, thank you Mother! Thank you so much. Is this the surprise you mentioned?"

Mother shook her head. A secretive glint lit up her small eyes. She smiled broadly. She seemed excited.

"I'm going out to get your surprise now," she said.

Chapter Two

Mother loves me. I listened to the sound of her locking and bolting the door and bit a chunk out of my apple, careful not to let any juice spoil my face. After tidying up my desk, I ran downstairs into the living room.

Mother owned a thousand or more books. Every week she turned up with a couple more. Most of them were adult books that I wasn't allowed to go near, but there was a small bookshelf next to the door connecting the living room to the hallway that was just for me.

The room was gloomy because of the wooden boards and navy curtains, the red sofa a murky brown in the darkness. I flicked on the standing lamp beside the rocking chair then walked over to my bookshelf. I saw the present immediately. There, on the end of the third row of books, was a book-shaped object wrapped in scarlet paper. I smiled and plucked the present off the shelf. Mother was feeling generous this year. Usually she gave me a small present like a new pen or a rubber, but this was a *book*.

In Mother's slanted hand read my name in capital letters.
MIRABELLE
Underneath my name were the words:
For a beautiful little doll who works so hard and behaves so well. All my love, Mother. P.S. You may open this now!

I tore into the paper and stared excitedly at the book cover. 'The Secret Garden' by Frances Hodgson Burnett. This was Mother's way of giving me a piece of the outside world. I half-smiled and lifted up the front cover. The pages were yellow with age and a little rough. I had a sniff. The book smelt intensely booky; good and musty. It was perfect. I curled my legs under myself in the rocking chair and lost myself in the story, escaping into another girl's world.

I was at the part where Mary Lennox meets a chirpy little robin, a bird which I had only ever seen in Mother's bird books, when I heard something. My heart seemed to jump into my throat. I held stock still. The sound was coming from toward the back of the house, but Mother wasn't home yet. I was home alone. No other living creature lived in the cottage. Just Mother and me.

Without moving, I trained my ears on the direction the sound was coming from. The sound was strange, unidentifiable. Uneven and raw. It was definitely not coming from the front door and it wasn't coming from upstairs, so it couldn't be the boiler having a meltdown.

I remained where I was for a while, my legs pinned under myself, eyes wide. I listened. An idea crossed my mind. *No*, I told myself, *you're not imagining it. You're not a little girl anymore. You know what's real and what's not.* But I thought about Polly and doubt crept around my mind like a sneaky rat. As a little girl I'd had an imaginary friend called Polly. Polly had looked exactly like me, but she'd been mute. I had played imaginary games with her whenever the opportunity arose and sometimes we just sat beside one another, keeping each other company. One day when I was six, Mother had said I was too old for her and told me I had to make Polly disappear from my head or she would. Worried about what Mother might do, I had ignored Polly until she had shaken her head sadly at me and vanished. I never saw her again, no matter how hard I tried to.

With a frown, I pushed myself up from the chair. *The sound is real. It's real.*

I had to see where it was coming from.

I tiptoed across the living room and carefully opened the door to the dining room. The noise was slightly clearer here. The pine floorboards creaked underfoot and I cringed and leapt through the door into Mother's kitchen. Again, the noise was louder in here - louder than before. My eyes fell on the kitchen blinds and I froze. The strange sound was coming from outside. Outside in the back garden. I was sure of it.

The blinds remained, as always, shut, drawn down over the wooden boards that had been nailed over the windows. Nailed firmly over the glass so no light could break in.

I had never heard anything from outside before. I had never been outside. Outside was too dangerous for me. I wasn't allowed outside and there were certain places in the cottage that I was not allowed to go. I wasn't allowed in Mother's room or in the spare room. I had never asked why these places were forbidden. Curiosity had always dangled on the edge of my mind but lately it had begun to push itself forward. I thought about the spare room. Mother had spent a lot of time in that room over the last few months but she wouldn't tell me what she was doing in there. I wanted to know but I didn't dare ask.

The strange sound from outside stopped. I stared at the blinds above the sink and listened. Nothing. Then I heard something else. I jumped as the front door slammed. Heard the locking and bolting of the door. *Mother's back.*

Without hesitation, I grabbed a glass from the cupboard and turned on the cold tap.

A moment later Mother giggled and I turned around, my heart thumping hard. Mother stood in the entrance to the kitchen wearing opaque sunglasses and a floppy sun hat. She carried a large black holdall in her sinewy arms. She placed the holdall on the kitchen table and looked at me. A smile spread across her face as she took off the sunglasses and hat and dropped them on the table.

"This is your surprise!" she said, spreading her hands wide.

"What is it?" I said, mustering up as much excitement as I could to conceal the frantic pounding of my heart.

She grinned. "Open the bag and see."

I put the glass of water on the counter and reached the table in two steps. Outside thankfully remained silent.

Mother leaned over the bag as I took hold of the silver zip and tugged, wondering why she had not wrapped the present. *She's probably too excited to,* I thought. The zip caught on the black material. I struggled to loosen it and Mother pushed my hands away.

"Let me do it," she snapped. She ripped the bag clean open and squealed excitedly, her hands balling into fists against her pale cheeks. "Look, Mirabelle, look! Isn't she perfect?"

I stared, unable to speak. Inside the bag lay a little girl of about four years old. She was curled up on her side, her tiny chest rising and falling steadily, her eyes closed. She had long, fair eyelashes that fluttered every now and then as if she was having a dream or a nightmare. Her hair was the same butter-blonde as mine, but curly rather than straight and no way near as long. Like me, her milky skin was freckle-free. She wore a pale blue dress, a white cardigan and sparkly, silver tights. There were no shoes on her feet.

"Isn't she perfect?" Mother repeated, stroking the little girl's cheek.

"Who is she?" I croaked.

"Her name's Clarabelle. Such a pretty name for such a pretty little doll, don't you think?"

I swallowed with difficulty, my mind racing. "Where's she from?"

"Utopia," Mother said dreamily.

I hesitated. There was a fiction book in Mother's bookcase called 'Utopia', which meant it couldn't be real. I swallowed. "Where's she *really* from, Mother?"

Mother's head whipped around, her hair spraying out like sparks of fire. She glared at me, nostrils flaring. "Don't you like her? Don't you like your present?"

I took a step away from the table. "I think she's perfect Mother, I really do. I just want to know more about her, that's all."

Mother's eyes narrowed and she tilted her head to the side. "If I tell you she's from Utopia, she's from Utopia."

I nodded and glanced at the sleeping child, a queer, sick feeling working its way up my throat like thick treacle.

"Thank you for my book, Mother," I said.

"That's fine. Tell me what you think of her, of Clarabelle."

Mother watched me intently. I looked at the child's face, thought about how oddly similar our names were. It could have been a coincidence, but I wasn't so sure. Mirabelle and Clarabelle.

"She's beautiful and, er, really small. She must be quite young," I paused, telling myself to be brave, "How old is she?"

"She's five," she paused, "I rescued her."

The sick feeling eased a little, "You *rescued* her?"

Mother nodded. She bent down and lifted the little girl out of the bag. Kissing the girl's forehead, she left the kitchen and walked through the dining room into the living room where she placed the child on the sofa and covered her with a blanket. I watched Mother perch on the edge of the sofa and stroke the child's face over and over again, a faint smile on her thin lips.

"If I hadn't saved her, she'd be dead right now," Mother said softly.

"What do you mean, Mother?"

"That's enough Mirabelle," she said, her tone sharpening.

She picked up the little girl and I watched her carry her out of the room. I listened to Mother's feet travelling up the stairs, heard her turn at the top. *She's taking her to the spare room,* I thought.

The spare room that I haven't been allowed in for months.

*

Mother came downstairs two hours later. Curled in the rocking chair trying to focus on my book, I looked up at the sound of her footsteps and opened my mouth to speak but she walked straight past the open living room door without glancing in my direction.

"Mother?" I said, rushing after her into the kitchen.

She slapped butter onto two slices of white bread, added spam then pushed one slice down on top. My stomach grumbled and I waited for her to hand me my sandwich, but she walked past me out of the kitchen with the sandwich in hand.

"Mother?" I repeated.

"I'm busy. You can make your own lunch. You're plenty old enough for that now."

I felt like I'd been slapped. She left the room and went back upstairs.

Mother always made me my lunch if she was home, which she usually was, and she always, always made me my lunch on my birthday. One year she put a candle in the sandwich and told me to blow it out and make a wish. That was on my seventh birthday. That year I had wished that Polly would come back, but of course she never did.

On my eighth birthday Mother had brought me a red cupcake covered with the most delicious white cream. When I had blown out the candle, I had silently wished to go outside into the back garden just once before I died. Mother had not given me any more birthday candles, but I had still made the same secret wish when I turned nine, ten, eleven and twelve: to go into the back garden before I died.

My shoulders prickled. A headache hummed in my temples.

I had not made this year's birthday wish yet. There was no point in wishing for the back garden because Mother had already said no. Perhaps when I was older...*if I live that long.*

I drifted toward the blinds. A layer of dust feathered each black, plastic panel. I drew my finger along the bottom panel and inspected the pad of dust on my fingertip. It was grey and furry. Mother's and my skin and hair and who knows what else was hidden in there amongst the million other particles of dirt and grime.

I rinsed the dust off my finger, my gaze lingering on the blinds. Behind those blinds lay wooden boards and behind those boards lay glass. Behind the glass lay the back garden, where the strange sound had come from. I listened intently and heard nothing. All was quiet out there right now. Perhaps it had been my imagination playing games, driven wild by my desire to go out there and experience another world.

I glanced at the kitchen door. It too was blacked out, boarded up, locked and bolted so no light could invade the gloomy interior of the cottage.

My chest twittered with the closeness of outside. There would be grass and flowers and maybe a robin, like Mary Lennox's robin. A creature I could talk to besides Mother, even though it could not talk back. Someone, perhaps, who loved me for being me.

Mother loves me.

But now she's got Clarabelle, she won't love you anymore.

No. That's silly. Mother rescued that girl. That girl's a stranger and Mother loves me.

"Mirabelle."

Mother! I whipped my head around but she wasn't there. The kitchen was empty.

I frowned, puzzled, scanning the small shadowy space, the abandoned hallway beyond.

I took a step toward the hallway then stopped. My headache was worsening. Stabbing pains set my temples on fire. I needed painkillers but Mother had the key to the medicine cabinet. She wore a set of keys on her belt every day. Said it was the safest way.

Before I could stop myself, I left the kitchen and crossed the hallway. At the bottom of the stairs I stopped. My head felt like it was cracking open. I had always suffered from headaches but this was the worst one yet.

"Mother?" I called. My voice came out small and pathetic.

I grabbed the banister, leaning against it as a wave of nausea swirled in my throat. I pulled myself up one step then another.

"Mother?"

Another step and another. Another and another and another. My head was splitting open.

I reached the top of the stairs and dropped my head between my knees, but that made the pain worse. I lurched into the bathroom and threw up in the sink, my whole body shaking, head spinning. All I could think was *This is the end. Mother's right. Dolls live short lives. I can't believe it's happening so soon. I can't believe I'm going to die in the bathroom on my thirteenth birthday.*

"Mirabelle! Are you alright?"

"Am I dying, Mother?" I croaked.

"No. Hush now, little doll. You're not ready to go. *I'm* not ready for you to go yet."

It was Mother at my side. Mother who was concerned about me. Mother who was rubbing my back and whispering reassuring words and unlocking the medicine cabinet and giving me painkillers and removing my makeup and helping me undress and running me a bath and tucking me up in bed and smoothing my hair back from my hot, damp forehead.

Mother loves me.

After a while, Mother closed my bedroom door softly and I closed my eyes against the pain, which was dying much more quickly than I thought it would. I remembered Mother's reassuring words and soft touch. Her worried eyes.

I slept.

Chapter Three

A mewling sound woke me. I sat up straight in bed and strained my ears. Someone was crying. Someone young. *Clarabelle.*

My head ached but the horrific pain from last night had receded. I got out of bed and crept toward the door of my bedroom. I tried the door handle, relieved to find it unlocked. Sometimes Mother locked me in without any explanation. Occasionally I heard a knock on the front door and realised she was locking me in to protect me from the outside. Other times I heard nothing and remained in my bedroom studying for hours before she came to let me out. The longest she had ever left me was six hours. The little gold clock on my desk had told me so. She had apologised that time and given me a big hug, which had made it all better.

The mewling sound was still audible so I crept out onto the landing and tiptoed toward the spare room. I felt sure that Mother would be angry if I spoke to Clarabelle without permission, but the temptation was too great. Mother was the only person I had ever spoken to and here was a living, breathing, *different* person. If I didn't take this opportunity, I knew I'd go mad with curiosity.

I hesitated halfway across the landing and listened, training my ears in the direction of downstairs. Nothing. Not even a whisper of Mother.

Go for it.

The grey carpet swallowed up my footsteps as I tiptoed the next couple of steps to the spare room. Ever-so-quietly, I knelt down and put my ear to the door.

"Clarabelle?" I whispered.

The crying stopped abruptly. The little girl said nothing, but I could hear her ragged breathing.

"Clarabelle? Are you okay? It's Mirabelle. I live here with Mother..."

There was no response, only a loud sniff.

"Clarabelle? Please speak to me," I whispered.

Silence. Another sniff.

"Please?" I said.

A few more sniffs.

I turned to go.

"My name's not Clarabelle," she whispered. Then she started crying again.

A shiver criss-crossed my shoulder blades.

"What do mean?" I said.

But the little girl would not answer. I repeated the question again and again to no avail.

Feeling strange, I whispered, "I'll be your friend. You can trust me." I looked at the door knob, thought about trying the door. If Mother caught me I'd be in so much trouble. She'd probably lock me in my bedroom for a week. Maybe more.

"I'll come back soon," I promised, hoping another

opportunity would come soon.

Mother was in the kitchen boiling eggs. She was humming to herself, her head bobbing along to her tune. It was a lively, fast tune I'd not heard her hum before. She was already dressed in her tight, blue flare jeans and an orange and brown flowery blouse.

I watched her for a moment feeling like a spy, noticing how light and springy she seemed. She seemed happy. Excited almost.

"Good morning, Mother," I said.

She whirled around, her eyes widening with surprise. "Gosh, you scared me!"

"Sorry."

"Let me just finish these eggs then I'll get my purse. We can't have you looking like something the cat's dragged in, can we, doll?"

I shook my head, noticing with a stab how she had not called me *little* doll.

We ate our eggs, buttered soldiers and salt in silence. I was about to eat my last mouthful when Mother's eyes focused on mine.

"You look awful, Mirabelle."

I looked down at my plate to hide my expression.

"You look twice your age," she added scornfully.

I gulped back the lump in my throat. "I'm sorry Mother."

She tutted, finished the last of her toast and took my plate away before I could finish my last bite.

"Go to the dining room. I'll be in in a minute."

In the dining room, I tried not to bite my nails. I was used to Mother's comments about my appearance but they seemed worse than usual today. Almost like she'd enjoyed saying those things and seeing my reaction.

Mother loves me.

Does she?

Of course she does. And you do look awful. Who wouldn't look awful after being so sick?

I stripped off my long white nightgown and knickers, hoping to please Mother with my readiness to be dressed and made up. But Mother did not come downstairs after a minute or five minutes or ten or even thirty.

I stood there shivering in the gloomy room that reeked of dead flowers, wondering what to do. I eyed the grandfather clock in the corner, the one that had always given me the creeps. It was huge and black and hideous with a gold-rimmed face and spiky gold hands. Mother said it had been her grandfather's. Said it was an heirloom. Her grandfather had died of heart disease but he had left the clock to Mother along with the cottage and everything else in it. On the wall beside the clock hung a black and white photograph of Mother when she was a little girl with a wrinkled old man whose face was fixed in a scowl. That was him. Her grandfather. My great grandfather. In the photograph, Mother was holding the old man's hand. She looked pretty in a frilly dress, her hair tied in sweet bunches, but her face looked sad. Her grandfather wore a suit. I eyed the photograph more closely, keeping as far away from the grandfather clock as possible.

What had always struck me as odd about the photograph was that someone had clearly been cut out of it, because a tiny hand about the same size as Mother's was tucked into the old man's other hand, but the person that the hand belonged to had been chopped off the photograph.

Mother was an only child and her parents had died when she was a baby, so maybe the person holding the old man's hand had been a friend of Mother's. Maybe that friend had died in a terrible accident. Maybe that was why Mother never mentioned who that hand belonged to, or even the fact that someone had been cut off the photograph.

There were so many maybes that my mind swirled with them.

"Have you taken your pill?" Mother's voice was sharp.

"Yes."

"Good doll."

She handed me a pair of knickers and I pulled them on quickly.

"Arms," she said.

Obediently, I stretched my arms up in the air so that Mother could pull my dress down over my head and onto my goose-bumpy body.

Today's dress was rich blue with a flouncy, white petticoat sown in underneath. Mother made all of my dresses. I had worn this one many times before and it was growing a little tight across my chest.

Mother stood back and assessed my appearance. A frown scrunched her forehead into crumpled paper and her small eyes shrank to brown peas. For a fleeting moment she was the spitting image of her grandfather and I shrank back, looking down at myself, wondering what I had done to earn such a disgusted grimace.

"Take it off," she snapped, "It's too small. You're...developing. It's disgusting. You're still a child for God's sake!"

I pulled off the dress with difficulty, ripping several hairs out of my head. Fortunately, Mother was too enraged to notice. Muttering under her breath she stomped upstairs and returned seconds later with an emerald green dress embroidered with pink flowers. She threw it at me and I pulled it on over my head, hoping desperately that it wasn't too tight. I hadn't worn this one for about a month. I exhaled, emptying my body of air to shrink my lungs. Mother eyed me suspiciously and tilted her head to the side.

"Yes, that's much better," she sighed. I could almost see the relief pouring out of her. She smiled and I inhaled a huge gulp of air. The room was silent for a second and then it was shattered by a ripping sound as a side seam tore open. Mother's nostrils flared and she grabbed the collar of the dress and ripped it off me, leaving me standing there trembling in my knickers.

"Run upstairs and put on the dress you were wearing yesterday," she barked.

I dashed out of the room and took the stairs two at a time. Tears dribbled down my cheeks and I swiped them away, determined to hold them in. I'd be in even worse trouble if I went back downstairs with tear-stained cheeks. My dress was in the bathroom in the laundry basket. I pulled it out, grimacing at the smell. It was still covered with my sick. I grabbed the bar of soap and ran the hot tap, desperate to clean the dress, but Mother was shrieking at me to hurry up so I abandoned my cleaning efforts and pulled on the damp, stinking dress and ran back downstairs. I lost my footing halfway down and nearly fell, my heart a hammer in my tight chest. The grandfather clock struck eight o'clock, booming the eight hours in a slow, mocking manner that made me want to punch its ugly face.

"I'm so sorry Mother," I panted, sitting down at the dining room table.

She ignored me and began to paint my face in a frantic, rough way, holding my chin with fingers like pincers, her jaw clamped shut, her eyes narrowed. This was not the tender, careful Mother I knew. This was another person. A person who was changing faster than I could keep up. And I knew what had kick-started this change. Clarabelle.

"Sit still," Mother snapped.

I wasn't aware I had moved. I sat extra still and focused on the navy curtains and what beautiful things might lie beyond. My chest began to relax and I floated in my imagination, picturing birds and trees and grass and flowers. Pretty, gentle things that I could admire. I pictured the sun and my eyes burned with tears that I could not let drop.

Mother finished with my makeup. I sat up straighter, eager to feel the slow, tender strokes of the hairbrush, but Mother packed up her purse and left the room without a word. I listened to her mounting the stairs, to her opening and closing the spare room door. The sound of her choosing to be with a strange little girl she'd only just met rather than me. I looked at the hairbrush that Mother had left on the dining room table. I picked it up and began to brush my hair in long, slow, gentle strokes, but it wasn't the same.

That was when it hit me: nothing was going to be the same ever again.

Chapter Four

I didn't know what to do, so I went upstairs and opened my grammar book. I had studied Mathematics yesterday so Mother would want me to study English today.

I sat at the desk and stared at the words. The text swam. My chest felt like someone was standing on it and my eyes stung with the effort of keeping salty tears locked inside my eye sockets. Stabbing pains pulsed in my temples. I picked up my pen and began the exercises. A tear dropped onto my page smudging the word 'friend'.

Mother loves me.

Love is reciprocal. Do you love Mother?

My door opened; I jumped and swivelled round, dabbing my wet eyes with my fingers.

Mother stood in the doorway. Her mouth was turned down at the corners and her eyes looked shiny. Over her arm she held one of her blouses. An orange one with a huge white collar and large white flowers printed all over.

"I'm sorry, Mirabelle. I overreacted. I'm just worried, that's all."

"Worried?" I said.

"Yes, I'm very worried."

"What about?" I ventured nervously, helping Mother remove the stinking scarlet dress from my body.

She sighed and rubbed her face. She looked tired. Old. Her hair was starting to grey at the temples and wrinkles clustered around her eyes and mouth.

"I'm worried about Clarabelle."

Part of me didn't want to hear about Clarabelle. I didn't want Mother to focus on her any more than she already did. Another part of me, the curious cat part, was hungry to know more about the mysterious arrival of this little girl who I never even knew existed before yesterday.

"Why are you worried?" I said.

Mother handed me the orange blouse and I pulled it over my head, grateful to be away from the stench of my own vomit. The blouse smelt of oranges, like Mother, who wore an orange-blossom moisturising cream every day. I'd asked if I could try it on once but she'd said no. Moisturiser was for grownups not little dolls.

Mother perched on the edge of my bed and I swivelled in my chair to look at her.

"Turn on the lamp. It's too dark in here," she said.

I switched it on, blinking to adjust my eyes to the sudden in-pouring of light. Mother's shadow loomed larger than life on the wall behind her. Her head looked huge, alien-like. I had read all about aliens in my science-fiction books. Science-fiction wasn't my favourite genre, but Mother liked me to read a bit of everything.

Said it widened my vocabulary and made me more interesting to talk to.

I waited for Mother to speak, wary of asking too many questions. If I asked too many questions she could close up or get angry and I would never find out more about the little girl in the spare room.

"There's something I haven't told you about grownups in the outside world," Mother said.

I waited, leaned forward a little, suddenly feeling very grown up myself.

She hesitated. Frowned. "Grownups can be cruel. *Very* cruel. They can have...vile sexual appetites."

I gasped inwardly, struggling to wrap my mind around the implications of Mother's words.

"You remember I told you about sex? About how babies are conceived?"

"Yes. But, I don't understand -"

"Clarabelle's father," she said, "he *abused* Clarabelle. He *abused* his own flesh and blood."

"That's why you had to rescue her!" I said, latching on at last.

Mother nodded and clasped her hands together on her lap. She sat up straighter and raised her chin. "If I hadn't taken her away from that vile man, I just know she'd have ended up dead in the mind – or worse."

"How did you know Clarabelle's father was doing those vile things? Did you see?"

Mother looked off into the distance, perhaps into a memory. "I'm very intuitive, Mirabelle, and when I saw the way he dragged her around the supermarket, I just knew. You know what I mean?"

I nodded, trying to understand, telling myself to look up the word 'intuitive' in Mother's mammoth dictionary later.

Mother stood up and grabbed my wrist. "Look, I'll show you."

I let her pull me out of the bedroom and across the landing. She released her grip on my wrist and wrestled with the keys at her belt. I watched her unlock the door, suddenly nervous. Did I want to see what was in that room?

But Mother closed the door behind her, careful not to let me look inside. She came out with a sleeping Clarabelle in her arms. Mother had changed her into one of my old white nightgowns. A bubble of envy surfaced in my mind and floated for a second. I shook my head as stronger feelings of pity and sorrow thrust themselves forward and popped the hateful bubble of envy. The little girl was a victim. An innocent, helpless child who had done nothing to deserve the vile actions of the person she probably trusted more than anyone else in the world. I wondered about Clarabelle's mother, but I didn't say anything.

Mother lay the little girl on the carpet at my feet and knelt beside her small body, stroking her cheek. The girl didn't stir at all. She looked peaceful, but I could see dried tear stains on her pale cheeks.

Mother pulled up the girl's left sleeve to reveal a horrible bruise on her tiny upper arm. "Look, Mirabelle, look! Look what that vile man did to her!"

The bruise looked like fingers - strong, angry fingers that had gripped the little girl's upper arm so viciously that blood had climbed to the surface, pooling under the girl's delicate skin like a handful of squashed plums under a piece of paper.

"That's awful," I whispered, "But, you've taken her away

from him now. She's safe, isn't she?"

Mother dragged her hands down her face. She looked like she was about to cry. She shook her head. "I'm afraid the damage has been partway done."

"What do you mean?"

"I mean, Clarabelle's mind. It's damaged. I think - I hope - given time, the damage can be reversed, but..."

"But what?"

Mother exhaled heavily. "She's not making sense. Her name, for example. She thinks her name is Emma, which of course is complete nonsense. It's a brain thing, you see. She's all confused because of what that vile man did to her."

"Does she need to see a brain doctor then?" I said.

"No, don't be so ridiculous," Mother snapped, "All she needs is my love and care."

I looked down at Clarabelle's small face and murmured, "I can help too. I want to help make her better."

Mother patted my arm. "Best if you stay away from her for now. Too many new faces will be all the more confusing for poor Clarabelle."

I nodded, trying not to feel hurt.

"Now, off you go back to your studies. I'm popping out to get some fabric to make Clarabelle's dresses but when I get back, I expect you to have completed all of Section B. If you finish before I get back, you may read your new book."

"Thank you, Mother!" I said, excited by the prospect of reading more of 'The Secret Garden'.

I walked back to my bedroom and turned to watch Mother pick up Clarabelle then take her back into the spare room. Mother was so kind, so good to rescue poor Clarabelle. She had taken it upon herself to take care of a broken doll and fix her, and the extra burden was clearly taking its toll on Mother.

At my desk, I tried to concentrate on subordinate clauses, but something niggled and gnawed away at my concentration. I had more questions about Clarabelle. The questions were attacking my brain and hurting my tummy. I tried and failed to crush them. Finally, I got up and did one hundred star jumps, part of my daily fitness routine. The surge of adrenaline boosted my mood a little and I did another hundred and twenty, stopping when my heart felt like it was going to burst. I went into the bathroom to use the toilet then ran downstairs to grab a glass of water. When I returned to the landing, glass in hand, I heard a quiet voice from the spare room.

"Hello?"

It was Clarabelle. She was awake. Her voice sounded wobbly but at least she wasn't crying.

I hesitated. Mother wanted me to stay away from Clarabelle. She had said 'too many new faces will confuse her'. That meant that as long as Clarabelle didn't see me, I might be able to help her feel better without confusing her and making her feel worse.

"Hi. It's me again. Mirabelle. How are you feeling?"

There was a long pause. I knelt down next to the door.

"Clarabelle?"

"My name's not Clarabelle," she stumbled a little over the name, "My name's Emma. Emma Hedges."

I frowned. She sounded so convinced. Mother was right. The little girl was very confused.

"Help me," she said beginning to cry, "I want my my my Mu-u-mmy."

I couldn't stop myself from asking, "Your mummy? Where

is she?"

"I don't kn-know."

"You're safe here. No-one will hurt you anymore. Mother will take care of you like she takes care of me."

Clarabelle's crying grew louder. My heart hurt; I hated hearing her so upset.

"We're going to be a bit like sisters," I said, trying to sound excited.

"I do-do-don't want you to be my sister. I want my Mu-u-mmy! I want my Mu-u-mmy!"

She began to scream that phrase over and over again. I tried to calm her down but her cries became more and more frantic. Feeling like I'd made her worse, I backed away from the door and shut myself in my room. I sat on my bed, hugged my knees and covered my ears, desperate not to hear the little girl's terrible screams and terrified that Mother would come home any second and realise what I'd done.

After about twenty minutes, the little girl went quiet.

I sighed with relief and carried on with my grammar work.

Chapter Five

At midday I went down to the kitchen to prepare my own lunch, as instructed. Mother hadn't said anything about preparing lunch for Clarabelle, but I made her a spam sandwich too. I also made one for Mother, cutting off the crusts carefully, just the way she liked.

Mother hadn't wiped down the kitchen which was odd as she was usually so vigilant about keeping a clean house. To be helpful, I washed the dirty dishes, dried them and placed them in their cabinet, hoping Mother would be pleased. The problem was that it was hard to predict how Mother would react. I often wondered if all grownups were like Mother. In my books some of the adults were always kind, calm and patient, but that was made up. That wasn't real life. That was the beauty of books: you could turn reality into anything you wanted it to be.

I was carrying Clarabelle's sandwich up the stairs when the front door rattled. I froze on the stairs feeling guilty even though I could not put my finger on what I'd done wrong. I ought to get out of there, away from the doorway where sunlight would be pouring in any second, but my feet were stuck to the carpeted stairs, my neck craned round painfully, my eyes following the movements of bags of groceries as they were flung in through the door, which was open about a forearm's width. I pressed myself flat against the cold wall, my eyes trained on the door, which swung open a few more inches every time Mother threw another bag inside. So many bags were piling up in the doorway that the door opened wider, allowing me a glimpse of light so blinding that I gasped and shielded my eyes. It felt like someone had just held a lit match a hair's width away from my eyes and yet I peeled my eyelids open under the protective shield of my hand and stared at the wonderful array of colours outside. I caught a glimpse of shocking blue – the sky, and green so vivid it stung – grass - and a rich, lush, bunch of dark green – bushes, I guessed. I saw slices of wood poking up out of the grass and I saw golden pebbles on the ground. I drank it all in, lapped it up, cared little that at any moment Mother would step inside and see me bathed in sunlight. I suddenly felt so high that I wanted to throw myself down the stairs, jump over the shopping bags and run outside.

But then reality reared its hideous black head and pain exploded in my brain. Mother was right. I was allergic to the outside, to the sun, to the lovely light, and I was going to die soon, sooner than I had to, because I had just sped up the process by allowing the light to get me. *Dolls live short lives.*

Panic and fear tore at my throat and I raced upstairs. Clarabelle's sandwich flew off the plate and landed in a mess on the landing. I knew I would be in trouble, but I had to get away from the light. I jumped onto my bed and grappled with my bed covers, pulling them over myself until I was submerged in darkness. My body shook and my head pounded. The pain was killing me. I was too hot under the covers. I shook them off and lay back in bed. Nausea swept up my throat but the sick feeling hovered there and my mouth did not turn to liquid so I knew I wasn't going to be sick this time.

Staring at the rough, white ceiling, I counted down from one hundred, slowing my breathing to match every other number. I could hear something downstairs, something amazing. I listened for a while and the pain lessened. Curiosity seemed to make the pain go away and my inner cat won.

Still feeling shaky, I padded out onto the landing and hastily gathered up the ruined sandwich. Tearing it into pieces, I flushed it down the toilet then went downstairs, trying to ignore a nasty stab of guilt.

Mother was in the living room dancing in front of a huge machine I'd never seen before. The machine seemed to produce the incredible sounds filling the house. The sounds coming out of the machine sounded like the tunes Mother hummed. *So this is what music sounds like.*

Mother had her eyes closed and her head thrown back. A dreamy smile played at her lips as she swayed her long, thin body to the music. I watched, mesmerised by her, transfixed by the peaceful look on her face. For a second, I almost didn't recognise my own mother.

"What's that?" I blurted before I could stop myself, pointing at the machine.

Mother laughed and opened her eyes. "It's a record player, silly. I got it dirt cheap at the car boot. Got a load of records for it too. Thought the music might cheer me up a bit. Help Clarabelle relax. I'd forgotten how great it feels to dance. I only listen to music in the car these days."

She showed me a bag full of huge black discs.

"These are records. They have music recorded onto them, then they go in the record player, which makes the music come out. Far out isn't it?"

I nodded. I tried to move my body to the music like Mother, but I felt too stiff.

"How do you do that?" I asked.

"Do what? Dance?" she laughed and grabbed my arms, "Like this, silly doll!"

She span me around and around and around. I felt my chest loosening and a smile sprang to my face. It was strange but smiling made my cheeks ache.

I laughed and Mother laughed. I felt like I'd been whisked to a fairy land. It was the best I'd felt for a long long time.

"Who made the music?" I said as Mother let go of my hands and I fell onto the sofa, my head spinning with dizziness.

"Only the best band on the entire planet. ABBA of course!"

"ABBA?"

She nodded enthusiastically.

"What is ABBA singing about?" I said, not sure what Waterloo was.

Mother frowned and stopped swaying. "That's enough questions, Mirabelle. You always ask too many questions."

She did something to the record player and the music stopped abruptly.

"I'm sorry, Mother, I didn't mean to -"

Without looking at me, she said, "Go upstairs and write a detailed description of something. I want to see how your control of tenses is progressing."

I followed her out into the hallway where she was grabbing

up bags and lugging them into the kitchen.

"Can I help, Mother?"

She shook her head and I watched her pace back and forth lugging bags.

"I made you a spam sandwich," I said, following her into the kitchen.

"That's nice," she muttered.

Feeling desperately confused about Mother's sudden change of mood, I picked up my sandwich and took it upstairs with me. At the top of the stairs I listened for any sound of Clarabelle. I heard a sniffling sound and took a tentative step toward the door. Before I knew it, my feet had carried me to the spare room.

"Hi, it's Mirabelle. Are you feeling any better?" I whispered, careful not to call her Clarabelle in case it upset her again.

I heard Mother's footsteps on the stairs and rushed into my bedroom. I thought about going out to talk to Mother, but I didn't want to upset her any more than I already had.

*

"I had a sister you know," Mother said, making me jump.

"What? I mean, pardon, Mother?"

I looked up from my description and leant forward in what I hoped was a casual, natural-looking movement. Mother leaned against the door frame, her eyes fixed on something far away. My arm obscured my work. I didn't want her to see it. Not yet. Not until I had decided whether to show her the description with my drawing or without it. Mother used to let me draw pictures to go with my work when I was little, but I was learning that the rules were different when you turned thirteen. Mother might disapprove of the fact that I had drawn a sketch to go with the description. Then again, she might not. I was beginning to realise that I could never be sure which way Mother would go. It was starting to make me more nervous but more careful too.

I distorted my face into a fake smile, trying to ignore the soft crying sounds coming from the spare room. If Mother heard them, she did not show it. I wanted to ask if Clarabelle had had any lunch but the words dried up on my tongue.

"Pardon, Mother?" I repeated, prompting her to repeat herself.

"I had a sister," she said dreamily.

"Really?" I sat up straighter. This was brand new information about Mother. The fact that Mother was opening up to me filled me with hope that I was not a lost cause. That I was not going to die - not soon anyway. *Mother still loves me.*

"Yes. Her name was Sarah. She was my twin."

"Your twin?"

My mind buzzed with this new information. Why had she not told me this before? If she had a sister, then I had an aunt. Why was Mother talking in the past tense? Was my aunt dead? But I knew better than to blast out loads of questions like bullets from a gun. If Mother wanted to tell me stuff, she would, in her own time.

"Yes," Mother said solemnly.

"Were you and her identical?"

"You and *she*," Mother corrected sharply.

"Were you and she identical?" I said.

She shook her head, her eyes glazing over. "We had the same blonde hair but she was a great deal more beautiful than I was. She looked like the most perfect little doll you could ever imagine. Everyone commented on her beauty. Complete strangers would stop in the street and give her compliments. Grandfather loved her for it."

She moved over to my bed and sat down, beckoning me to join her. I got up from the desk and perched on the edge of the bed and she patted her lap, like she used to when I was little. I lay down and rested my head on her thighs, looking up into her face, thinking about how difficult it must have been for Mother, being the ugly duckling and always being second best.

The knots in my chest loosened and began to unravel as Mother's fingers lightly stroked my forehead. She had not treated me so lovingly for a while now. Tears bubbled up but I suppressed them by focusing on the angular cut of Mother's jaw, the way it moved as she talked.

"Sarah was perfect," Mother repeated, "Grandfather thought she was an angel – his angel - and he spoiled her rotten. On the outside she looked so innocent and sweet and lovely but on the inside she was pure evil. Rotten to her core.

"After breaking his leg fighting so bravely in the first war, Grandfather went into the oil industry – that's where he made his money. When my parents died in the car crash, he retired and came back to look after us. We were only two years old at the time. We were a handful but Grandfather raised us all by himself. My grandmother had died ten years previously. Grandfather was a faithless man after that – rare for that time – but he was also traditional, like me. He was a good man, most of the time..."

Mother trailed off like she was lost in thought. Lost in memories. I was desperate to know more. Questions scratched at my throat like sandpaper. I wondered what Mother meant by 'most of the time'. There had seemed a dark tone in her voice when she had said the words.

I waited a few beats then asked my question, "Did Sarah...die?"

Mother's fingers stilled on my head. "No," she said sharply, "She ran away."

"Ran away? Why?"

Mother looked down at me suddenly. From this angle her eyes looked cross-eyed, her nose sharp, her cheekbones blade-like.

"Because she disgraced us. Her evil actions shamed the whole family. She knew that if she stayed, Grandfather would kill her for what she'd done."

"Gosh! What did she do?" My mind span with ideas: robbery, kidnapping, murder...

Mother looked back up and shook her head bitterly. "That's another story for another day. I don't want you getting worked up and being sick again."

Without any warning, she stood, making my head jerk forward then flop back onto the bed.

I lay there thinking. I longed to know more about my evil aunt Sarah and my great grandfather. I dashed after Mother onto the landing and watched her walk to the spare room, unlock the door and disappear inside.

I sighed, disappointed, my tongue sizzling with questions, but then an idea popped into my head. I looked up at the panel in the ceiling, the one that led to the attic, and began to think. I had never been in the attic before so I didn't have the foggiest about what secret treasures lay up there, no doubt hidden beneath dust and cobwebs and many other gross, disturbing things, but a tingling feeling in my chest made me feel certain that at least one answer lay above my head, shrouded in darkness, waiting to be uncovered.

The thought gave me hope and I latched onto it like a leech. I did not want to die. What if...what if...

I couldn't complete the thought because I didn't know what I was trying to think, but I returned to my bedroom with a spring in my step, a plan forming in my head. If I was going to die soon, I wanted answers before that happened. I wasn't a little doll anymore. My name was Mirabelle the Curious and I was going to investigate. I was going to be brave and bold like Terrible, Horrible Edie and Mary Lennox and all the other heroines I had read about. I was going to discover more about my aunt and my great grandfather, and maybe even something new about Mother. If I didn't, I had a nasty feeling that the cat in my brain would claw its way out and get me in a whole grave full of trouble.

I sat down at my desk and smiled, excited by my plan.

Mother had never said I couldn't go up into the attic.

Chapter Six

The front door banged shut and the key crunched in the lock, signalling Mother's departure from the cottage and unlocking the rising hysteria that was gurgling inside me. Mother was gone. Gone shopping for groceries and maybe a few more books. Gone for how long, I did not know.

I could never be certain, but on average Mother's trips into the outside lasted two hours. On occasion, of course, they hovered around the six hour mark, but these lengthier excursions were few and far between, so I could not bank on her being out for anywhere near that long. Clarabelle was quiet, which was good. Perhaps she was asleep. I had seen Mother go into Clarabelle's room this morning holding a syringe. Mother loved Clarabelle, so I assumed the syringe had been full of some calming medicine that would help Clarabelle adjust to her new way of living. I felt sorry for Clarabelle. Even though Mother had rescued her from a nasty family, Clarabelle had been torn abruptly from everything she'd ever known. I wondered if she used to go to school every day. Did she have a best friend who she missed? Did she miss her school teacher? In many of the books I read, teachers were portrayed as unkind and mean. But in some stories, the teachers were lovely. Maybe Clarabelle's teacher was lovely. Maybe her teacher had been a source of comfort to poor Clarabelle when she had been beaten by her father. I couldn't help thinking that perhaps Mother had taken matters into her own hands a little too soon by bringing Clarabelle here and making her part of us. But who was I to interfere? I knew very little about the outside. I only knew fragments; things that Mother told me.

Can I trust Mother? Does she always tell the truth?

I shivered. I ought not to be entertaining these thoughts, especially as I was about to betray Mother's trust in the worst way. Mother had never said no to the attic, but I knew she wouldn't want me up there. Just because she had never said the rule out loud, that didn't mean it did not exist.

Guilt glued me to my chair. I looked at 'Othello', the Shakespeare play I was supposed to be reading. The tiny words blurred into indecipherable spiders' legs – thousands of them. Black, spiky, harsh. My heart thumped in my chest and a cold sweat broke out under my arms. I should not go up into the attic. I should be a good doll and do as I'm told. I had never gone against Mother before.

Dolls live short lives.

No. Go up there. Investigate. Stop being such a wimp!

I hurried out of my bedroom onto the landing before I could change my mind.

Plunged in shadow, the landing looked more unwelcoming than ever – a cold, grey void that lay below a possible wealth of treasures. I looked up, just imagining, the curious cat scratching relentlessly against my skull. Beyond that small door in the ceiling lay answers, I felt suddenly certain of it.

I stood on tiptoe and reached up to the small brass knob. My fingers skimmed cold metal. I was too short, which was hardly surprising. I had nothing to compare myself to, but I only reached up to Mother's chin and Mother told me that dolls usually stopped growing at about thirteen years old. Mother measured me every year. When she last measured me I had been exactly five foot tall, and I had weighed seven stone. I did not know Mother's precise height. And I never asked.

My tummy started to hurt, low down, and I laid my hand on it. It felt rock hard – with tension probably. I wasn't used to betraying Mother's trust. I knew better than to be so stupid and yet here I was, standing beneath the attic, about to do something I knew deep down was against Mother's wishes. But I had to know more. There were things I needed to know and if Mother was not willing to tell me...well, I was going to die soon anyway, so did it matter if I disobeyed one unspoken rule?

The sick, unthinkable feeling that always flooded me when I thought about dying erupted in my chest. It was overwhelming. All-encompassing. Horrifically frightening. Terrifying and incomprehensible. This fear was worse than the fear of what Mother might do to me, should she ever find out, which I was determined wouldn't happen. If I stopped dilly-dallying, I would be up and out of the attic before Mother came home. I was wasting time. There was a perfect word for what I was doing. It began with a 'p' and hovered on the tip of my tongue and mind. I was p...pr...pro...procrastinating! I was dragging my heels – no – more than that – I was putting off the inevitable. I had already made up my mind. I was going up there.

I dragged the chair out of my room and placed it in the centre of the landing, directly underneath the attic door.

Cramps roiled in my tummy. I ignored them and stepped up onto the chair. Now I could easily reach the brass knob, so I turned it and pulled. The door opened easily but with a loud creak. I glanced at Clarabelle's door and strained my ears; all remained quiet. The end of a ladder was in reach, so I pulled at it tentatively and it slid down and out of the darkness like an uncoiling snake. I jumped off the chair, ladder still in my hands, and nudged the chair out of the way with my shoulder. It promptly fell over, thudding onto the carpet. My heart thundered, but there was no noise from Clarabelle's room; she was heavily asleep. Thank goodness.

Shuffling backwards, I pulled the ladder down until its feet met the carpet and the ladder was fully extended. I gave it a push, checking it was secure. I had never seen Mother go up into the attic. If she had not used this ladder for many years, there was a chance that termites or damp had rendered the wood dangerous, but it seemed sturdy and I didn't weigh much. Visions of Mother returning to find me in a heap on the floor, my body twisted like a discarded, damaged doll, flickered in my mind's eye. But if I fell, I fell.

A steely kind of determination settled itself in my mind, and I ascended the ladder with slow, careful movements. Each rung creaked underfoot and hand and gave way a little, but not much.

I reached the top of the ladder and stared into a pit of shadows. Biting my lip, I braced myself, fearful of creepy-crawlies that might be lurking on the walls, and felt along the wall for a light switch. There was no point going inside if I couldn't see anything. My fingers touched string and I tugged. Something clicked and a naked bulb came on emitting a low buzz. The bulb was weak but it did the job. I glanced around the attic, my eyes greedy. Attic floors could be unstable, I knew, so I gingerly stepped onto the floorboard in front of the ladder, relieved to feel nothing give way, the wood cool beneath my bare foot.

An unpleasant smell circled me. It was an ancient, mouldy, moth-eaten kind of smell that made me wrinkle up my nose and breathe through my mouth as I stared in horror at the masses of cobwebs that hung between the wooden rafters like Gothic, lace drapes. The roof was not far above my head; if I stretched my arms up, my fingers would touch those grotesque cobwebs, no doubt inviting a hoard of hungry spiders to crawl down my arms and underneath my dress where they would feast upon my skin with their tiny, needle-sharp fangs...

Ugh. I shivered and turned my attention to the contents of the attic.

I counted eight cardboard boxes, one filthy mattress and two leather trunks. There was a lot of stuff to search. It was going to take me all day, maybe longer, to go through everything. But I didn't have all day. I didn't even have two hours.

Gingerly testing each part of the floor with an outstretched foot, I made my way towards the closest box. The box, like all of the other boxes in the attic, was a plain cardboard box big enough to fit me inside if I were to curl up in the foetal position. It was smothered with dust and contained lots of grubby, dusty, old books. I picked up a few, surprised to find them written in another language. Latin perhaps. I was careful to check for spiders before picking anything up. I sneezed three times and more dust clouded the air.

One box down, seven to go.

I had been up in the attic only about ten minutes so far giving me quite a bit more time before Mother came back. Hopefully.

I pulled open the second box and stared. It was full of photo albums. I picked up the top one and blew off the dust. The moment suddenly felt so big that I stopped breathing. Something tickled my arm and I screamed and stared in terror at the enormous, big-bodied spider on my right forearm. For a moment I was paralysed. I dropped the album and flicked the spider off my arm with my free hand. My skin crawled and I rubbed my arm frantically, desperate to be rid of the lingering feel of its spindly legs on my skin. A shiver of revulsion pulsed through me. I exhaled shakily and looked down at the album, which had fallen open to the middle.

Taped to the page was a black and white photograph of two girls who looked about the same age as each other, perhaps nine or ten years old, holding hands. One girl was a lot prettier than the other with a rounder, more symmetrical face and a small, delicate nose. The pretty girl smiled at the camera but the other did not. Both girls were dressed in identical frilly dresses and wore their hair in matching bunches. I brought the album close to my face and stared more closely. Both girls' faces were painted like mine. I recognised the plainer girl as Mother. The other girl must have been Sarah. Mother's twin sister. My evil aunt. Except, she didn't *look* evil. If anything, it was Mother who looked a bit...

A banging sound interrupted my trail of thought. Mother was home!

I left the album where it was, leapt over the box, scurried back to the attic door and scrambled down the ladder, heart twittering frantically. My feet found carpet and I seized the ladder and hoisted it up. It was heavy but it slid up, up, up...and then I couldn't push it any further up because I was too short.

I froze, listening for Mother, but all was quiet. Had it been

Mother I'd heard or had I imagined the distant banging sound?

Gently, I slid the ladder back down until it rested on the ground. I tiptoed up to the banister and peeped over the edge down at the front door. The door was shut. Mother was not back yet.

I exhaled a whoosh of hot breath and rolled my eyes at my own stupidity. I was on edge and had simply imagined the sound, a bit like I had the other day in the kitchen.

I looked at the ladder. Now that I was on the landing, I found it impossible to make myself go back up into the attic. How long had Mother been gone? It could not have been more than twenty minutes surely?

I padded into my bedroom and checked the clock. Yes, Mother had left twenty-two minutes ago. She would not return yet. Hopefully.

But my heart still hammered in my chest and my palms sweated. That noise had given me an awful shock. I stood and listened. Nothing. I must have imagined it.

Deciding all was safe, I climbed up the ladder and retraced my footsteps.

I found the album and turned the page.

The next photograph was of the pretty girl lying naked on a bed. A strange, sick feeling entered my throat. My fingers hovered on the edge of the page. The girl was perhaps two years older than she had been in the previous photograph. Her eyes were wide with what looked to me like terror. She lay flat on her back like a star, her small wrists and ankles tied to the corner posts of the bed.

I could not make sense of what I was seeing. The girl's face was painted like mine. She looked like me. I scanned every inch of the image, but there was no trace of Mother in the picture.

I did not want to turn the page, but I had to.

I turned the page and my hand flew to my mouth. Mother had told me about sex, so I knew what I was seeing. Anger twisted inside me. *No. No!*

Unable to stop myself, I flicked the page to the next photograph and bile rose in my throat. I closed the album with a loud slap and shook my head, trying to dispel the horrific things I had seen. My mind struggled to process everything. I closed my eyes, clenched my hands into fists. I knew what that was, but I did not want to admit it. Aunt Sarah could not have been any older than me in those pictures. My great grandfather had hurt Mother's sister, Sarah. Had he hurt Mother too? And who had taken the photograph of him doing that?

One more question circled my brain like a bird of prey: why would Mother keep this obscene album? This...*evidence*.

The only explanation was that Mother did not know it was up here. I stared around the attic with new eyes, unable to search any other boxes, unable to forget what I had seen. That poor, poor girl. Mother had warned me about the evil that lurked in men. I thought about poor Clarabelle. How she too had been abused by her own father. No wonder Mother had rescued her; she had seen the same terrified expression in the little girl's eyes and known, instinctively, what that evil man was doing to her. It was clear now that Mother had also been abused – but why had she said that her grandfather was a good man? It didn't make sense. Unless Mother was so traumatised by everything that things had grown muddled up in her mind. Poor Mother. Poor poor Mother. And here I was, disobeying her.

I rushed away from the foul album and tripped over a box. My hands and knees thudded onto the floorboards and I screamed as a nail plunged into the palm of my hand. I wrenched up my hand and gaped at the hole in my skin, at the blood rising up like water out of a flooded drain. How would I explain this to Mother?

Frantically, desperate to keep the blood away from my dress, I searched the attic for a piece of fabric, cloth, anything to stop the bleeding. Then I spotted it. Poking out of one of the trunks was a blue bit of fabric. I picked my way over to the trunk and knelt down. With my left hand, I lifted the trunk lid. Inside the trunk lay a pale blue dress that looked big enough for a toddler. I grabbed the dress and wrapped it around my bleeding hand. I tied the sleeves of the dress into a tight knot around my wrist and sighed, racking my brain for things to tell Mother about how I cut myself. For *lies*. Guilt sliced across my tummy and I sighed again. Poor Mother.

I moved to close the trunk, but something caught my eye. Poking out from beneath a small yellow dress with white hearts printed all over it, was a piece of black and white paper. A sliver of newspaper.

I plucked the paper out from under the dress and lay it flat on my knees. My hand throbbed. The blue dress was already blood-soaked but I ignored the pain and stared open-mouthed at the newspaper cutting, blood draining from my face.

I could not move. Blood dripped through the blue dress onto my knees. My dress was ruined. Mother would be furious. But I still could not move.

Chapter Seven

I sat down on my bed and stared at my bloodied hand. I had untied the blue dress, put it in a bin liner and shoved it deep into the kitchen bin underneath all of the other rubbish. My hand had stopped bleeding, but it was covered with congealed blood. I had not bothered to rinse it. For some strange reason, the sight of all that blood was comforting.

Through blurry eyes, I re-read the newspaper article. It could not be true. I could not bring myself to believe it. *Mother loves me.*

There had to be an explanation for it. There just had to be. There was no way Mother would do that to me. To anyone. Newspapers got things wrong all the time, didn't they? Newspapers lied. Made up stories to make money. This was one big, fat lie. There was not a single bit of truth to it.

I had carefully closed the lid of the trunk, switched off the attic light and descended the ladder in a dreamlike state. Standing on the chair, I managed to restore the ladder to its folded up position inside the attic then I had shut the attic door. Mother would never know I had been up there. She would never know what I had seen. She need never know what I had found out. I could go on as normal. Tell myself it was all a lie. Tell myself Mother was still Mother. The Mother I had always known. That Mother had rescued Clarabelle. That Mother loved me.

To believe the article was to believe a great many terrifying things. Things that destroyed every piece of my world. But to believe in the article, was also to believe in a tiny glimmer of hope that I might not be on the verge of dying. To believe in the article was to believe that I might live to the ripe old age of eighty. I might not have to face the terrifyingly final hand of death for a long, long while to come.

The front door sounded. I folded up the article and tucked it inside my pillow case.

Mother loves me. Mother would never lie to me.

"Mirabelle?" Her voice floated up the stairs into my bedroom. It sounded so familiar, so *her*.

I curled myself over. Hugging my injured hand to my stomach, I croaked, "Mother?"

"Mirabelle? Mirabelle!" she was coming up the stairs now, her footsteps heavy and angry, her voice sharp.

"In here, Mother," I whispered.

The door burst inward and she rushed toward me, "Mirabelle! What happened?"

"I cut my hand," I said.

"How? On what? What on earth were you doing?" she demanded, crouching down in front of me.

I shrugged. Tears dripped down my cheeks onto my bloodied lap. I saw Mother take it all in; my spoiled face, ruined dress, torn hand. I could not bring myself to lie to Mother. But I would not tell her exactly what had happened.

Mother stared at me. A frown furrowed the space between her eyebrows. I waited, sniffed, tried not to hope too hard that she wouldn't get mad. Her eyes darted all over my face and dress. Her lips pursed and she shook her head.

"Poor little doll," she murmured.

She left the room then returned with a laundry basket. She helped me remove my dress and dropped the soiled material into the basket then led me to the bathroom where a hot bubble bath was running. The mirror steamed up and the soothing fragrance of orange-blossom saturated the warm air.

"This is a sign," she said darkly, to me or to herself I couldn't be sure.

She checked the temperature of the water then helped me step into the bath. Immediately, my muscles relaxed and the cramps in my tummy eased.

"Keep your hand out of the bubbles," she instructed, her tone gentle.

I watched her leave the room. Mother was not furious. She was being loving and kind. Mother would never lie to me.

Mother loves me.

The article was a lie. There was no need to say anything or do anything about it. Mother need never know.

She came back in and cleaned my hand with disinfectant, her movements slow and soft, her brow creased with concern.

I watched her bandage my hand. She knew what to do. Mother always knew what to do. She had trained as a nurse before she had me. Nurses cared for people. A nurse would never do anything bad. Mother would never do anything bad.

"There," she said, "Now tell me what happened."

She moistened a cotton wool ball in the bath water and gently removed my makeup.

I closed my eyes, enjoying the sensation of soft, warm cotton wool stroking my face.

"Mirabelle, tell me."

My eyes snapped open. Mother continued to wipe off the makeup but the pressure she applied was more forceful. Panic nibbled at my insides.

"I, um, fell," I said, staring at my hand, hoping she could not hear the sudden frantic pacing of my heart.

She continued to wipe my face. The pressure lessened a little.

"You fell?" she prompted.

I stole a glance at her eyes. They were fixed on a space above my head. Zoned out almost.

I cleared my throat. "Yes. I went to the bathroom and when I was coming out, I thought I heard a noise downstairs, so I ran downstairs and I tripped and fell and my hand slammed down onto something sharp on the carpet."

There. I'd lied. Guilt exploded in my chest. The bath suddenly felt too hot.

"Mother, can I get out now please?"

She nodded and left the room without saying a word.

Worry chewed and gnawed at me, but I pulled out the plug and climbed out of the bath. I wrapped a towel around myself and dried my feet on the bathmat before going out onto the landing. Mother was unlocking Clarabelle's room.

"Mother?" I said.

Either she did not hear me or she pretended not to. She went into Clarabelle's room and closed the door. I moved closer to the room. Was Mother angry? Why had she left so suddenly? I made my way to Clarabelle's door and put my ear to the wood. I could hear Mother whispering loving, soothing things to the little girl. In that moment, a sharp pain twanged in my heart. I longed to be that little girl again. That perfect, innocent, unspoiled child who believed everything Mother said and who, in Mother's eyes, was a perfect little doll who was not about to die.

I turned and walked back to my bedroom. Dried blood soiled my bedsheets. I slowly removed the sheets and retrieved some fresh ones from the airing cupboard. I did not change my pillowcase.

Suddenly exhausted beyond tears, I got into bed and tried not to think about the newspaper article underneath my head, but it was impossible.

*

I woke up, surprised to find that I had fallen asleep. My head felt groggy and my hand throbbed. I pulled on a nightgown and went downstairs as quietly as I could, unsure where Mother was, unsure whether she was angry with me. I did not know how long I had slept; if I had slept against Mother's wishes, she was sure to be cross.

"Mother?" I said when I reached the bottom of the stairs - the stairs I had used in my lie.

There was no sound, no response, so I crossed the hallway and entered the living room, my heart jolting as I took in the scene.

Clarabelle sat at the table in my seat and Mother sat beside her, painting her face. The dead roses were gone, the vase empty.

"Mother? I'm sorry."

Mother did not reply. It did not even seem as though she had heard me.

I approached the table. "Mother?"

"Yes?" she said, continuing to paint the girl's face.

Clarabelle's eyes moved to mine. Her eyes looked sleepy.

"I'm sorry I slept for so long. I didn't mean to."

"That's alright. Sit down and wait your turn. I'll make you up in a second. I've nearly finished Clarabelle."

Relief burst in my chest and I sat down, happy to wait, grateful Mother still wanted to paint me.

"There!" Mother said, clapping her hands and beaming at Clarabelle, "Isn't she beautiful? Such a pretty little doll. Now what do you say, Clarabelle?"

The little girl yawned. She looked so strange with all that make up on.

"Thank you," she said groggily.

"Thank you, *what*?" Mother said sternly.

"Thank you....Mother."

"That's better. Good little doll."

Mother proceeded to brush Clarabelle's long blonde hair. I watched, fighting a creeping sensation of unease. Why was Mother telling Clarabelle to call her Mother? I thought about how Clarabelle had insisted her name was Emma. Emma Hedges. I thought about the similarity between our names. Mirabelle and Clarabelle. Was it a strange coincidence or was the little girl's name really Emma? And why did the child seem so groggy today? Just a few days ago she was screaming for her mummy and now she was behaving like this. So calm and obedient. Was it the medicine Mother had given her in the syringe? Was Mother...I could not complete the thought. Guilt tussled with reason and fear.

"Go back up into your bedroom now Clarabelle. I'll be up to tuck you back into bed soon. I know it's morning but you need to rest."

Clarabelle obediently left the room. I watched her go. She moved slowly and sluggishly, as if invisible weights were tied to her ankles pulling her down.

"What's wrong with her?" I said.

Mother's eyes narrowed. "What on earth do you mean?"

I swallowed, regretting my words. "Nothing, Mother."

"She's just tired, that's all. When you've been through something like she has, you become tired very easily."

I nodded.

Mother picked up her red purse.

I looked down, feeling something wet between my legs. Mother's eyes followed mine. She screamed and jumped up from the table.

"You filthy girl! Go and wash yourself. Stuff your knickers with a flannel. I knew this was going to happen soon. I just knew it!"

"What? Oh, have I...have I started my period, Mother?"

"Yes, but you're not a woman! You're supposed to be..." she trailed off, waving her hand at me, "Never mind. Just get out of my sight. I can't bear to look at you like this. I knew your time would come. I just hadn't imagined it would be so soon."

"But, Mother? Please! What are you saying? Am I going to die?"

She buried her face in her hands. Her whole body shook. "Get out! Get out! GET OUT!"

I stumbled backwards out of the room. I ran upstairs and shut myself in the bathroom, chest heaving, heart pounding, confused and frightened. I had read a book called 'Are You There God? It's Me, Margaret' a couple of months ago which had a bit about some girls starting their period. I had asked Mother about it at the time, surprised and pleased that she was letting me read such a grown up book. She had told me not to worry, that I would never get a period because little dolls didn't get periods. But now I had got one. A period. Was that bad in real life? Was it another sign that I was dying?

I did as Mother had told me as quickly as I could and then went into my bedroom and changed into one of my prettiest dresses, hoping Mother would approve, that seeing me looking like her little doll again would calm her down.

"Mother?" I said, hurrying downstairs, "Mother? I did as you asked. Mother?"

Mother ignored me. She moved away from the record player as ABBA's music blasted into the room, the volume so loud it hurt my ears. A song called 'Our Last Summer' pounded against the walls. I noticed the red purse on the floor in the middle of the room, its contents spilled over the carpet.

"Mother?" I said.

She closed her eyes and swayed to the music. Tears rolled down her cheeks. Without looking at me she pushed me backwards out of the room and closed the door, shutting me out.

Chapter Eight

I sat on my bed and stared morosely at the wall. Mother refused to talk to me. She would not even look at me. She had begun to act like I didn't exist. I knew I had done wrong by sneaking up into the attic, but Mother didn't know I had done that, so that could not be what was making her so angry at me. In my aching mind, I replayed her reaction to the blood between my legs. That was what had made her so angry, and yet that was not my fault. According to the book I had read, every girl's body did that sooner or later. To bleed was natural. It meant I was developing properly. It was a sign that I was entering puberty and my body was preparing for pregnancy. It was not, I told myself forcefully, a sign that I was dying.

   I thought about the evil photographs in the attic and Mother's disgust became slightly more rational; seeing me develop could have reminded her of the terrible things her grandfather did to her and her sister when they were about my age, and maybe even after that. It outraged me to think that my great grandfather could have done that to Mother and Sarah at all, but I knew in the back of my mind with some horrifying certainty that he would have done those terrible things more than just that one time. Mother was very likely traumatised by her past. I had to be more understanding, more compassionate. If I showed Mother the sympathy and tenderness she deserved, maybe things would go back to normal.

I spent the morning reading 'Othello' and trying not to wince every time I heard Mother and Clarabelle. They were downstairs together. I think they baked a cake, because the delicious smell of warm sponge floated into my room.

At lunchtime, I went downstairs into the kitchen. I was right: Mother and Clarabelle sat at the kitchen table together eating slices of jam sponge.

"Good afternoon, Mother," I said quietly.

Mother ignored me. She smiled sweetly at Clarabelle, who stared sleepily up at me. Jam dripped from her lip onto her chin. I glanced at Mother, saw her eyes narrow angrily at Clarabelle's mistake. Clarabelle had ruined Mother's careful work. I poured myself a glass of water, expecting to hear Mother tell her off, but Mother did not utter a word.

"Mother?" I tried, taking a small sip.

She smiled again at Clarabelle, licked her finger and tenderly wiped the jam off the girl's chin.

"Mother? Please. I know why you're so upset. I-"

"Leave us," she snapped.

"But Mother," I said urgently, stepping up to the table, "I can help you. I want to help."

Mother slowly stood up and walked around to stand in front of me with her back to Clarabelle, who stayed sat at the table eating her cake.

In a harsh, lowered tone, she stabbed her finger into my chest, "I said *leave us*. What, exactly, do you not understand about that simple instruction?"

My chin trembled but I sucked in a breath and whispered, "I know what he did to you. I know why you're acting like this."

"What?" she snapped. She seemed half-angry, half-puzzled now.

"Your grandfather. I know what he did to you. And, and, to Sarah."

The moment I said 'Sarah', Mother went crazy. She grabbed my hair in her fist and dragged me out of the room. I saw Clarabelle jump up from the table, her little face pinched with fright.

"Mother, please! I just want to help you. I love you!"

I tried to pull and twist away but I couldn't. Mother dragged me to the front door and pushed my face against the wood.

"Is this what you want? Is it?" she screamed in my ear.

"What? I don't understand!" I gasped.

"You want me to kick you out? Out there? Where the light will burn you from the outside in? You want that, do you?"

"No, Mother, no! Please. I'm sorry. I'm so, so sorry."

But Mother wasn't listening. She unbolted the door, unlocked it and opened it an inch. She shoved my face toward the opening; I scrunched up my eyes and tried to resist but she was too strong.

"Please don't. I'm sorry!" I sobbed.

There was a moment of silence, then Mother actually laughed. It was a short, sharp laugh. A laugh that suggested she was enjoying this.

Her grip on my hair loosened. She brought her mouth to my ear and whispered, "If you want to stay here with us, inside where it's safe, you will keep your mouth shut, do what you are told and you will never, ever mention her name again. Is that understood?"

I nodded. Silent tears streamed down my cheeks.

She let me go and pushed me backwards. I stumbled onto the stairs and fell on my back.

Mother closed and locked the door, threw me a disdainful look then walked away toward the kitchen, singing sweetly, "Little doll? Why don't we read a story together? Wouldn't that be nice?"

I stared at her retreating back, lost in a whirlpool of emotions, but there was one emotion battling against the fear, misery and confusion that I had never really felt before. Anger.

Chapter Nine

I shouldn't feel angry at Mother. Mother was coping with things in her own way. She was simply trying to protect me, make me understand. Light was deadly to me. And there were men out there like her grandfather who would want to hurt me. It was no wonder Mother had always told me the outside was so dangerous.

But she laughed at you. She enjoyed tormenting you. And if she really loved you, would she do what she just did to you? Would she threaten to send you outside into the deadly light if it really was deadly? And the light didn't kill you that time when you were on the stairs and Mother started throwing bags through the doorway. Think about the article. Think.

No. Stop it.

I pushed myself to my feet and leaned against the banister. Mother's voice floated out of the kitchen and along the hallway to my ears. She was reading to Clarabelle. It sounded like she was reading 'Terrible, Horrible Edie'. A wave of sadness washed over me, then I wondered if Mother had chosen that book on purpose.

'Terrible, Horrible Edie' had been my favourite book since I was eight. Edie had a dog called Widgy. I had always wanted to ask Mother if we could get a dog, but I had never screwed up enough courage to ask. Edie was the gutsiest girl character I knew and she never felt guilty for her actions. But I wasn't gutsy. I was boring and well-behaved, just how Mother wanted me to be. Except...

A smile tugged at my lips and a spark of victory danced across my guilt: the attic. I had gone into the attic. That was really naughty. Pretty gutsy too.

Stop. Stop being bad. Mother is hurting. Think about what he did to her when she was little.

But I didn't want to think about it. Thinking about it brought images into my head that made me have sick, bitter feelings I'd not experienced before. I was glad he was dead, but puzzled. Why would Mother say he was a good man when he had done those awful things to her?

Shaking my head, my long hair swishing like a mermaid's, I tiptoed down the stairs and crept along the hallway. The kitchen door stood slightly ajar. Mother's voice was sweet. Loving and tender. Lilting and expressive. In that moment, I yearned to be her perfect little doll again, to be treated like the only thing that mattered. Special. Her special, perfect little doll. My heart hurt and my knees buckled. I nearly collapsed. I leant against the cupboard under the stairs and listened.

Mother turned her voice into Edie's feisty, ten year old one and said: "If you start going to sleep," said Edie, "I'm going to pinch you."

Clarabelle giggled then yawned – a huge, long yawn.

I heard Mother's chair scrape, the fridge open, liquid being poured into a glass. Glug, glug, glug.

"Drink your milk then you're going back to bed for a sleep."

"I don't want to," Clarabelle said, her voice small and whiny, "I want to go outside and play."

"You can't. I've already told you this," Mother's voice was steely.

"Why? I want to go play. I always go play."

"Clarabelle. Look at me. Look. At. Me."

Clarabelle sniffed.

"You can't go outside because it's dangerous."

"Mummy never says it's dangerous," Clarabelle said quietly.

"Well...Mummy isn't well, remember? That's why you live here now. I'm your new mummy. I'm your mother and you must listen to Mother."

There was silence. I heard the grind of object against object and guessed it was Mother sliding the glass of milk across the table.

"Now drink this and then go upstairs. Hurry up now or there'll be no more stories."

"If I wear a hat, can I?" Clarabelle persisted.

In my head alarm bells belted out a manic tune. I cringed. This could only lead to disaster. Clarabelle didn't know it yet, but Mother did not like resistance of any kind and Mother always, always got her way.

A horrid beat of silence followed.

"Fine," Mother said.

I jerked in surprise.

The chair scraped; she was getting up. "If you want to go outside, go outside. Here, I'll unlock the back door for you."

"Yes!" Clarabelle squealed. Her chair scratched at the floor. She too was on her feet. I heard her skipping, skipping toward the back door.

The key crunched in the lock, but the door did not open.

"You may go outside as long as you're prepared to feel the most pain in the world," Mother added solemnly.

The skipping stopped. "What do you mean?" Innocence. Confusion.

"If you go outside you will get hurt very, very badly. The light will hurt you."

"But it never hurt me before..." Doubt crept into her voice. Fear simmered there too.

"Yes, I know, but you're poorly just like your old mummy. She got ill and gave her illness to you so now you can't go outside into the light anymore. Light will hurt you, Clarabelle."

"But what if I wear a hat and gloves?"

"No. It won't work. The light can travel through clothes and when it does it will kill you, but first you will go through a huge, horrible amount of pain."

"What will the light do to me?" Clarabelle said, sounding more curious than upset.

"It's too horrible to say," Mother said. She locked the door. I heard the jangle of keys.

"Tell me. I want to know."

"I'm not sure I should tell you. You might be too young..."

"I'm not. I'm five!"

Mother chuckled. "Ummm..."

"Please! Please, please, please, please!"

"Tell you what. You drink your milk then I'll take you upstairs for your nap and I'll think about it."

"Does that mean you'll tell me when I wake up?"

"Maybe."

"Please?"

Mother laughed. "Maybe. Now, drink up like a good little doll."

Clarabelle swallowed her milk noisily. She yawned again. Footsteps headed my way. I darted across the hallway into the living room and hid behind the small bookcase. They walked upstairs slowly, Clarabelle trying to guess what the light would do to her – *will it make my eyes sting? Give me a headache?* And Mother saying *Oh no, worse than that. Much, much worse...*

Crouching down behind the bookshelf like a frightened rabbit, I stared unseeingly at the navy curtains. First the name. Clarabelle. Three syllables. Ending in 'belle'. Belle meant beautiful. I knew that from 'Beauty and the Beast'. Dolls were supposed to be beautiful. I was Mother's doll. Now Clarabelle. Painted puppets on strings. Marionettes marching to Mother's instructions. Obedient, trusting.

Read the article. Read it properly.

No!

To trust or not to trust?

Mother loves me.

Does she?

I dashed over to Mother's gargantuan bookcase. It loomed large and intimidating, full of millions of pages, billions of words. Imagination crammed between slivers of leather. My eyes scanned the shelves. Each row was dust-free, the lip of each shelf glossy and dark. Mother wiped and polished the bookcases every day. Even now the scent of wood polish tinted the air. Mother cared for her books almost as much as she cared for her dolls. Us. Clarabelle and me. In that order now it seemed.

There it was: Mother's huge Medical Encyclopaedia. I wasn't to go near Mother's books, but I needed to know. I had to put this devilish uncertainty to bed. If Mother was telling the truth and I was allergic to light - and Clarabelle was allergic to light – it would be in here, in this mammoth book. Newspapers were biased, Mother had taught me all about them. But Encyclopaedias were non-fiction. Pure fact.

I wiggled out the large book from the bottom shelf between the Oxford English Dictionary and Roget's Thesaurus. The book was so heavy that I had to kneel on the carpet and rest it on my knees. My fingers scurried over the pages to the index section at the back of the huge tome. The pages were thin and slippery but smelt comforting. For me, books had a perfume of their own. Warm, musty, exciting. *I'm a bookworm and a booksniffer - a bookdog.* I had a good, long sniff. This Encyclopaedia was about ten years old so quite new, but it smelt good and booky, and it would be full of modern, up-to-date science I could trust.

In the index I found the word I was looking for: allergy. I trailed my finger down the allergy sublist looking for 'light' but it wasn't there. I carried on down and spotted the word 'sun'. Sun allergy, pages 222-225. I hastily flipped to page 222 and immersed myself in information about 'Solar Urticaria' (SU). SU was a rare condition in which exposure to ultraviolet radiation, or sometimes even visible light, induced a case of hives that could appear in both covered and uncovered areas of the skin. That sounded like the condition Clarabelle and I had! I lingered over the word 'rare' for a few moments – disturbed by the idea that rare meant very few people in the whole world could have the condition. The words 'too much of a coincidence' skittered across my brain, but I read on, desperate to know SU's symptoms and effects.

Generally, the areas affected are exposed skin not usually protected by clothing; however, it can also occur in areas covered by clothing. Areas constantly subjected to the sun's rays may only be slightly affected if at all. People with extreme cases will also have reactions to light bulbs that emit a UV wavelength. Parts of the body only thinly covered can also potentially be subjected to an outbreak.

Life with SU can be difficult. Patients are subject to constant itching and pain, as within minutes of the initial exposure to UV radiation a rash will appear. If vast areas of the body are affected, the loss of fluid into the skin could lead to light-headedness, headache, nausea and vomiting. Extremely rarely, patients have been reported to experience an increase in heart rate that can cause a stroke or heart attack due to the body cavity swelling. Other rare side effects can be bronchospasm and glucose instability issues. Also, if a large area of the body is suddenly exposed the person may be subject to an anaphylactic reaction. Once free of exposure, the rash will usually fade away within several hours; rare and extreme cases can take a day or two to normalize depending on the severity of the reaction.

What on earth were bronchospasm and glucose instability issues? And what was an anaphylactic reaction? I flipped to the back of the book again, found bronchospasm, flicked to the right page. I couldn't really understand what it was, just that it made breathing difficult. I found out that glucose meant blood sugar and guessed that glucose instability meant unstable amounts of sugar in the blood – why that would be a problem I couldn't guess, but I didn't have time to look it up. It didn't sound that bad anyway – definitely not as bad as the broncho thing.

I sensed Mother. Any second now she would come running downstairs and I would have to shove the Encyclopaedia back in its place and act normal. Unable to stop myself, I located the page about anaphylactic reaction. That sounded serious. Enough to kill a person if not treated by a doctor straight away. Was this what Clarabelle and I had? Was that why Mother wouldn't let us outside? I swallowed, flicked back to page 222, hesitated, tore it out.

"Mirabelle?"

Footsteps thudding downstairs, moving quickly. Urgently.

Mother was coming. She knew I was up to something. And I was. I was being gutsy for once. Breaking the rules. Mirabelle the gutsy had come out to play.

Thud, thud, thud.

My heart flipped. I stuffed the page down the front of my dress and frantically shoved the huge Encyclopaedia back into its place.

Thud, thud.

It got wedged in, half-sticking out of the shelf.

Thud.

I gave it another push. The book slid in an inch but still protruded more than the books beside it.

I swivelled on my knees to face my bookcase as she strode into the room, eyes aflame.

Chapter Ten

"What are you doing?" She fired out the words, sharp with accusation.

Trying to find out the truth.

"Nothing Mother. Just looking at my books."

I could feel the crumpled page against my collarbone, thought for a horrible moment a corner of paper was visible out of the top of my dress.

Her eyes darted away from mine. She scanned the room quickly. I held my breath. Her eyes fell on the immense bookcase and she wandered over, raking her fingers through the hair on my scalp as she passed. The touch was not pleasant but not unpleasant. I wanted her to comment on how silky my hair felt, but she didn't.

"Shall I go upstairs and study?" I said. I stood up, glanced at the Medical Encyclopaedia, at its traitorous position. Wished I'd given it a harder shove.

Her fingers danced across the shelf second from top. Tap, tap, tap across Agatha Christie's spine. She hummed to herself –

ABBA, I knew – apparently lost in her own thoughts. I was going to be lucky. Her focus wasn't on me. It was on her beloved books. I turned to leave the room.

"Mirabelle?"

I stopped. "Yes Mother?"

"What were you really doing in here just now?" Her voice sounded dreamy, faraway, detached. That voice made warning signs bounce off the walls.

My heart skipped. Be gutsy. Lie.

I bit back rising guilt. "I was looking for 'Terrible, Horrible Edie'. I felt like reading it again but I couldn't find it."

She turned and walked away from the bookcase toward me, her steps slow, eyes unfocused.

"That's because I'm reading it to Clarabelle," she said, stopping to stand in front of me.

She reached out and tucked my hair behind my ear. A tender gesture. I wanted to like it but her touch suddenly felt odd to me. Strangely false. Like the touch of someone trying to comfort a stranger.

"It's a great story. I'm sure she loves it," I said, "Shall I go to my room and study now?"

Eyes still glazed, she murmured, "Yes, off you go."

I tried to walk normally as I left the room. I mounted the stairs at a steady pace. As soon as my foot touched the landing carpet I hurled myself into my bedroom and shut the door. My hands shook slightly as I withdrew the page from my dress. I sat down at my desk, slid my textbook out of the way and lay the page out on the desktop, flattening and smoothing out the creases best I could. Solar Urticaria. It sounded more like a planet or a star than a rare medical condition. Rare. That word again. It didn't say how rare –

like one in a hundred or one in a thousand – just *rare*. But how rare was rare? How young was young?

I re-read the symptoms and flashed back to that moment on the stairs. When I had seen the light, a headache had come then I'd thrown up. Those were two of the symptoms of SU. But...I read the passage carefully. It was only if light touched you that symptoms developed. You didn't get headaches and sickness from simply seeing the light. Hang on – yes you did - *sometimes even visible light, induces a case of hives that can appear in both covered and uncovered areas of the skin.* Did I get hives? What were hives? I guessed hives were some kind of rash. Yes. That made sense. But I didn't notice a rash on my skin. There could have been one though, but I was too busy throwing up at the time to notice any weird patches on my skin.

Why would Mother lie?

The question made me look up from the page. I winced with guilt.

Because the article is telling the truth.

No. Mother loves me.

Suddenly I knew what I had to do. My heart pounded. *You're going to die soon anyway, so you might as well.*

Before I could talk myself out of it, I turned on my lamp and held my hand directly under the bulb – not close enough for the heat of the bulb to burn as it would burn anyone, just close enough to see if my skin would react oddly. The light illuminated my hand making it look sickly yellow. I counted to thirty. Nothing. No redness, no swelling, no burning sensation and definitely no rash. I held my hand there for another thirty seconds. Another thirty. Nothing. No change in my skin at all. No itching or burning or anything.

Relieved, I exhaled and turned off the lamp. Inspected my hand again just to be sure. My skin was absolutely fine. That meant, according to the Encyclopaedia, that I did not have an extreme case, which also meant that I was very unlikely to experience the other awful symptoms I had looked up. I frowned. If I didn't have an extreme version of the condition did that mean light exposure would not kill me? With a sudden jolt, I realised something else: nowhere in the text did it say that SU made you die young. According to this information, as long as you stayed out of sunlight, you did not run the risk of dying. So...why did Mother always say that dolls lived short lives? Was there something else wrong with me? Some incurable disease she'd never told me about? I shook my head. No.

I nibbled on my nail, realised, stopped. Mother would be mad if I ruined my nails.

Suddenly I felt like screaming and hitting my fists against the walls. I stood and paced the small room, panic licking me like searing flames. My eyes fell on the heavy, sludge-brown curtains that were nailed into the wall. The centre of the curtains was sown together in a neat cross-stitch. I had never tried to unpick the centre of the curtains of course, but now I wondered. Were boards nailed over the windows behind the curtains or was there nothing but glass behind the heavy brown material?

Be brave. Find out. But take precautions.

There was a pair of nail scissors in the bathroom. I hurried out of my room, retrieved them from the bathroom cabinet then stood staring at the centre of the curtains. If I unpicked the curtains Mother would see what I'd done next time she came into my room. But I had to know.

I pulled a yellow doll dress out of my wardrobe and lay it on my desk. Trying to steady my trembling hands, I took hold of the centre of the curtains and began to snip through the very centre stitch. There were a good fifty stitches holding the curtains together. I cut open the first one and wiped sweat from my forehead. Good. One down, tons to go. I snipped through the next and the next, biting my lip, struggling to keep from shaking. Every few seconds I glanced at the door, certain Mother would rush in.

With five stitches snipped, the curtains still revealed nothing. Each curtain kissed the other protecting me from what lay behind. Unsteadily, I placed the nail scissors on my desk and picked up the yellow dress, wrapping it around my hands. I took a breath, shuffled my body to the side out of the path the sunlight would take when I parted the small unpicked space in the curtains. If there was no wooden board behind I would be subjecting myself to real light. I exhaled then pulled the curtains apart. My heart sank to my feet. Disappointment curdled with fear. There was no glass, just wood. Mother had made certain I was protected – *or unable to get away.*

My last thought rocked me to my core. I let go of the curtains, grateful to see them fall back together. It didn't even look like I'd picked some of the stitches out. Mother would only notice if she inspected them closely and why would she? They had held fast for my whole life. They were a permanent feature of my bedroom. My life. My short, short life.

I wondered if Clarabelle's room was the same. Mother must have boarded up her window too. That must have been why she had spent so much time in the spare room prior to Clarabelle's arrival.

Something in my mind clicked. My eyes went wide. My tummy lurched.

Mother had prepared the room for Clarabelle. Mother had known Clarabelle was coming here *before* that day in the supermarket, *before* she had seen Clarabelle and known she was being hurt by her father and known she had to rescue her. Did that mean...

I couldn't, *wouldn't* complete the question.

The article. Read the article.

I sat down at my desk. Determined to ignore that voice, I tried to get on with my work. I relaxed one moment, comforted by the knowledge that I was being a good doll, and frowned the next, distressed by questions that surfaced in my mind every few minutes, forcing themselves to be heard and leading me to a very dangerous, exciting idea.

Chapter Eleven

Mother went out an hour later. The door slammed shut, louder than usual I thought. Maybe she was angry with me again. Did she suspect I'd lied earlier? Was I going to be punished when she got back? I shivered at the thought. Would it be a week's silent treatment again?

I thought about going to Clarabelle's door, seeing if she was awake. No – Clarabelle needed to sleep and Mother would be cross if I disturbed her.

But Clarabelle was only a delaying tactic. I was never going to go and talk to her. I had already made up my mind.

I left my room and slowly descended the stairs. I knew I was going to go through with it. Dread was unfurling in my chest like a huge black demon hand and I let it. The hand closed on my heart and squeezed and squeezed. I felt like I couldn't breathe but I also felt that if my heart didn't slow down, I would have a heart attack. I imagined Mother coming home to find me sprawled on the floor clutching my heart, my eyes rolled back in my head, froth dribbling out of my mouth. She would be so upset. She'd dash over to me, hold me in her arms and sob. She'd tell me how sorry she was, how much she loved me, how I was not going to die...

Guilt gnawed and nibbled at my heart, but a creeping, dreadful sense of certainty lived in my head now, and it was beginning to thrive. I had to know the truth. I desperately wanted to believe in Mother; to believe anything else was to shatter my world as I knew it.

But it will also mean you're not dying. That you're not allergic to outside. And what's so good about a world of locked doors and boarded windows?

They tussled: the need to believe her and the desire for her to be lying. The need to know and the desire to remain ignorant.

I entered the living room, walked to the rocking chair and dragged it over to the living room doorway to face the front door. I picked up 'The Secret Garden' and sat on the rocking chair, setting the swing in motion with a light push of my feet. The chair creaked comfortably. I'd sat on this rocking chair so many times but never in the living room doorway in the direct path of the front door.

I was in position now. All I could do was read my book and wait for Mother's return. When she opened the door, everything would become clear and I would finally know the truth. Even if it killed me.

Chapter Twelve

The grandfather clock struck six 'o clock, droning the hour in its loud, rough voice. The sound tugged me out of my book. I looked round at its hideous face and wondered where Mother was. She rarely stayed out this late.

I re-read my last paragraph. Mary was about to show Colin the secret garden. I couldn't wait to see Colin's reaction.

Then I heard it. A crunchy growl of wheels. A grumbling engine. The slam of a door. She was right outside, right now.

My heart flip-flopped and I placed my book on the floor beside the rocking chair and stood up. The front door clicked and I jumped as it inched open and a band of light raced toward me across the floorboards. As the door opened wider, the band grew, stretching across the floor and lengthening, running diagonally across the narrow hallway toward the living room door and me. The light was white. My eyes tingled but I fixed my gaze on that ever-growing light. The door stood open about a hand's width and remained in that state. The light had not yet reached my feet. I looked down at my bare toes. They were an inch away from the band of sunlight. All I had to do was lift one foot and take a step forward and I would know. But fear was my enemy and sucked my courage away. I stood, frozen to the spot. Behind me the rocking chair still rocked, creaking on and on and on.

A bag flew through the front doorway. I stared at the brown paper bag as it tried to stay upright, then fell onto its side. A red apple rolled across the floor escaping the collapsed bag, only stopping when it hit the wall to my left.

Mother will kill me when she sees me standing here.
Not if the light kills you first.

Clarabelle's voice came from above sending loud, frightened cries through the ceiling that pierced my heart and gave me courage.

Another bag and another thumped onto the floor and the door opened some more. I stepped forward. I felt light on me. Warm, lovely light. I swam in it. I waited for the pain, the rash, the headache, the nausea, the vomiting. My heart pumped hard and fast but nothing happened. I stepped forward, making sure I was totally enveloped by light. Took another step. Another two bags landed on the floor in front of my feet. I raised my hand, took hold of the door, pulled it wide open and stared at the outside. Sun hit me. My eyes burned with tears. Mother lunged at me, pushed me back screaming and cursing, eyes shocked, but worse – enraged.

She slammed the door shut, locked it, pocketed the key. I lay on the bottom steps of the stairs where I fell. Other than a bruise on my back from hitting the stairs, I felt fine, giddy in fact.

"What the hell are you doing?" she screamed.

I smiled up at her, too happy to respond.

She slapped me across my face. Hard. Once, twice. My eyes

focused and tears streamed. Mother had never hit me before.

"I'm sorry Mother – I just – I don't know what got into me! I just wanted to know what it was like and I kind of got mesmerised and then my feet were pulling me toward the light and I couldn't stop myself."

I looked up, conscious of my face, how I must look. My makeup must be ruined. My eyes were probably red from crying.

"You look awful. I expect the light will be working its way into your veins right now," she said, leaning over and bringing her face close to mine, "Yes, I can see it. Oh you poor, silly doll."

My hands flew to my face. "What? What can you see?"

"The disease of course, spreading through your body, contaminating your skin. Killing you."

She sighed and dragged her hands down her face.

"Killing me? No – I feel fine. It doesn't hurt. I'm fine. Look," I showed her my pale, smooth arms.

She shook her head. "It doesn't show there, but on your face. And inside. Inside your body things will be happening now. Terrible things."

"Please – what's wrong with my face? Terrible things – what things?"

"Your organs will be starting to melt into one another and other, even more horrible things will start to happen."

Her eyes glinted. She turned her face away and I noticed her lip curling up on one side into a half-smile. A thought hit me: was she enjoying this?

"You need to be punished for what you've just done," she said.

I said nothing. My face felt fine, but I wanted to see what she was talking about. Was she lying or was something happening to my face? Had I just carved my own coffin?

Mother shook her head and turned away from me completely, waving her hand. "I can't bear to look at you right now. At what you've done to yourself. You disgust me. Go to your room. I don't want to see you for the rest of the day and there will be no dinner for you tonight."

I sat on the step, frozen for a moment. She walked away, leaving me alone.

Heart pounding, I scrabbled up the stairs on my hands and feet and ran into my bedroom, flicked the lamp on and faced the mirror. I stared, horrified. Not horrified by a rash or anything like that, but horrified by Mother's cruelty. There was nothing wrong with my face. Other than a slightly pink handprint from where she'd slapped me and two black streaks of mascara, my face was absolutely fine.

The light had not hurt me. I was not dying.

The sudden sense of certainty was overwhelming.

Mother is lying. Mother has been lying for a long, long time.

I slid a trembling hand inside my pillowcase, pulled out the newspaper article and read.

Chapter Thirteen

Girl, Three, Goes Missing in Salisbury

Polly Dalton was last seen at Sainsbury's in Salisbury on Saturday

Police are searching for a missing three-year-old girl who they suspect was abducted in a supermarket near her home in Salisbury.

Polly Dalton was last seen in Sainsbury's car park standing beside a red car in Salisbury on Saturday afternoon. The missing girl's mother, local teacher, Jane Dalton, 25, said she realised her daughter was missing when she reached for her hand in the supermarket and she wasn't there. "I was talking to an old friend and took my eye off Polly for a second. She must have wandered off when I wasn't looking." Polly's father, local veterinarian, Peter Dalton, 27, was at home when the incident took place.

Local shop assistant, Rebecca Birch, 16, said she saw a little girl matching Polly's description in Sainsbury's car park. Birch said: "She was standing next to a red car. I think she was talking to someone in the car but I couldn't see who it was."

Salisbury police said they were becoming "increasingly concerned" for the missing child's safety and have deployed a large number of officers to investigate the disappearance. Detective Chief Superintendent Frank Jones said police were following a number of lines of inquiry. He said: "Salisbury police have launched an intensive search and criminal investigation into the abduction of a three-year-old girl, Polly Dalton, in Salisbury. Polly was last seen in Sainsbury's car park at around 2.30pm. We are obviously becoming increasingly concerned for her safety and are asking for anyone with information to please contact us."

Hundreds of local residents in the large town were said to have joined the hunt for Polly on Saturday with many continuing their efforts overnight. Up to 200 people congregated at Salisbury Cathedral, as news of the apparent abduction broke, to help in the search for the missing girl.

Petrol station owner Tanya Khan said she re-opened her station on Saturday night to help with the search. Khan said: "My father called to ask if we would open so people could get petrol to help in the search. Locals are out in full force searching for her." She said some people had returned home overnight, but were planning to continue their search at 6.30am. "It just shows the community spirit of the town and how people get together in a crisis to do anything they can to help."

Police released two pictures of Polly and urged anyone with information about the child's disappearance to come forward. Locals have also put up posters of Polly around the town as part of their search efforts.

Harry Taylor, who works at The Haunch of Venison on Minster Street, said the pub was empty on Saturday night with many of the locals joining the search. "All the locals are looking for her in this area," he said. "Police are still looking." Taylor said police officers were "everywhere" and they were also searching cars.

I was abducted. Ab. Ducted. Such a weird, horrid word. I stared at the newspaper article, willing it to be a pack of wicked lies, knowing it wasn't. The air in my room seemed to close in around me making it difficult to breathe.

My real name was Polly Dalton. I had named my imaginary friend after myself. How strange.

I frowned at the article, at the black and white photograph of me, smiling. A three year old me. Pieces of the puzzle were slotting into place. I thought back to my earliest memory. It was of Mother and me making a cake together when I was four. I had no memories of my real parents who were apparently called Jane and Peter Dalton. I was taken from the supermarket when my mother's back was turned. Clarabelle was in the supermarket when Mother found her. Mother stole Clarabelle too. The story about Clarabelle's father was probably a lie. Mother – I had to stop calling her that – she wasn't my mother.

A wave of sorrow rolled through me and I curled up on my side on the bed and hugged my knees to my chest. My whole life so far was a lie.

I sat up abruptly and swivelled around to look at the boarded up window. I picked up the article and brought it right up to my face. In the background, behind my three year old self, stood a house. I was outside...I was outside and I wasn't dead! She had lied about that too.

What her grandfather had done to her must have made her lose her mind; he had damaged her when she was little, twisted her sense of right and wrong, because there was no right in what she had done to me. She had taken me from my real parents. She had locked me inside this cottage for the last ten years of my life and made me think I was dying. Made me believe I was allergic to the outside. She must have destroyed my family's life.

I wanted to scream and smash my fists into the walls, but I didn't. Instead, I stared hard at the picture of me - innocent, happy me. Polly. I liked that name. No. I *loved* that name.

My anger receded as my body began to shake. I got under the covers and turned onto my side. My body shook uncontrollably and my breathing lost track of itself. Short, sharp, ragged breaths wheezed out of me, and I squeezed my eyes shut and counted down from one hundred. I wanted to call for Mother, but she was no longer my mother. It was becoming harder and harder to breathe. I was hot, too hot.

It will pass. It will pass. Just breathe.

I pushed off the covers and counted down from one hundred again and again and again.

Finally, breathing became easier. I opened my eyes and stared at the ceiling. I tried not to think about all that I had discovered, but my brain reeled with all of it.

I was Polly Dalton. I was not allergic to the outside. If I walked out of the house right now, I would not die. I was not on the verge of dying. That too was a lie designed to...I swallowed thickly...*control* me. Everything was so wrong, and yet everything suddenly all seemed so right, so true. So horrifically sensical – if that was even a word.

Indecision glued me to the bed. I fought an overwhelming sense of loss and helplessness and tried to think of the future. The next step I took was crucial. Now that I knew Mother was who she was, an infinite realm of what ifs rose up, each one as unsettling as the next.

Chapter Fourteen

I could not, would not hurt her. My eyes strayed to the huge, wickedly sharp chopping knife lying on the kitchen counter. Until two days ago I had believed her to be my mother. There was a big part of me that wanted to carry on believing that but when I looked at Clarabelle and thought about my real parents and about the fact that I could go outside, I knew I didn't have a choice but to accept that the woman I had always called Mother was not my mother. She was a damaged person who probably needed help. She was a victim but she had made me her victim, and I needed to get away. My hand was healing and I felt like I had a plan. It was clear she had taken great care to keep me her dirty little secret. I had no idea where the cottage was in relation to any other buildings, but I suspected it was far from anywhere and anyone. Mother had invented a reason to keep me inside away from prying eyes and it seemed she was content to do the same thing to Clarabelle.

In my mind, there was no chance that she would respond to

reason. For the last two days she had acted like I didn't exist, which I found inexplicably painful, but her unkindness made what I was about to do that much easier.

I stood on tiptoes and opened the top kitchen cupboard where Mother kept the tinned food. If my plan was going to work, I might need some supplies. The last thing I wanted was to successfully escape the cottage then starve to death. The thought of leaving the cottage was unnerving but exciting too. For so long, I had dreamt about the outside world. About the wonderful, beautiful, colourful things I would be able to see and touch and smell.

Mother's voice drifted into the room from the living room. "You can't go outside, Clarabelle, little doll. It's far too dangerous."

"Why?"

"You're poorly, little doll. That's why your pretend mother gave you to me. But don't worry. Mother will protect you. Mother will keep you safe. Mother will never let anything bad happen to you. Mother loves you."

"Oh yeah. I forgot. Can we dance?" Clarabelle said, seemingly happy to accept Mother's lies.

ABBA blasted into the cottage and I relaxed a little, and pulled a tin of beans out of the cupboard. I dropped it into a laundry basket then grabbed a tin of sweetcorn. Laughter reached my ears and my heart burned. I kept putting tin after tin into the basket. When I had eight tins, I picked up the basket and crept up to the kitchen door. The hallway was clear. Another track started to play. This one was about a dancing queen. I dashed past the open living room doorway and caught sight of Mother and Clarabelle holding hands and spinning around together. Clarabelle saw me. My heart leapt into my throat and I turned and bounded upstairs, arms burning from the weight of the tins. I kicked open my bedroom door and pushed the laundry basket under my bed. Pulling the covers over the edge of the bed, I turned to see my kidnapper standing in the doorway.

Her face was red, her hair wild. Her small eyes took in my unmade bed and messy appearance. I wore her favourite dress but it was uncomfortably tight across my chest and stomach. I had not brushed my hair and of course wore no make-up, as that was her obsession.

"What were you doing just now? Were you spying on us?"

I said nothing. I didn't know what to say. My brain felt like a scrambled egg.

"I suppose you feel left out, do you?" she said, stepping into the room.

Again, I didn't reply.

"Poor Mirabelle. I know it's been hard on you since I rescued Clarabelle, but you can't let jealousy ruin you. Jealousy killed the cat you know."

"Curiosity killed the cat," I blurted stupidly.

Her eyes narrowed and she tilted her head to one side, trailing her eyes up and down my body and face, her lips twisted.

"Are you *correcting* me?"

I shook my head. "No – I – sorry."

"Sorry *what*?"

The words tasted sour on my tongue, "Sorry, *Mother*."

She stared at me for a long time, her jaw clenched. A large blue vein throbbed in her forehead. Finally, she sighed and said, "Good. Now, the kitchen's a mess and Clarabelle and I need lunch. Go and make us some sandwiches."

"Yes, Mother."

She nodded curtly and left the room humming.

I hastily moved the contents of the laundry basket into the back of my wardrobe behind my nightgowns then I placed the laundry basket outside her bedroom where I had found it. I hurried downstairs and made her, Clarabelle and myself a spam sandwich, which I gobbled down quickly before taking theirs in to them. They both sat at the dining room table. Clarabelle smiled up at me when I placed her sandwich in front of her. I was pleased to see that Clarabelle did not look as sleepy as before. Mother ignored me.

Knowing I did not have much time, I hurried back into the kitchen and grabbed the tin opener and a fork out of the drawer. There was nothing I could do about water because there were no empty bottles and if I emptied one out, she would notice straight away, so I took a mug from the cupboard then ran out into the hallway, past the dining room, past the living room and upstairs. If I found a stream, I could fill the mug and drink that way.

I deposited my treasures inside my wardrobe along with the tinned goods then hurried back down to hear Mother calling my name.

"Mirabelle! Come and clear away our plates."

I almost rolled my eyes, understanding what was happening; from now on she was going to treat me not like her precious little doll but like a slave. My doll-like status clearly had an expiry date. Anger bit, made me nauseous, but I obeyed her instructions and cleared away their plates, which I washed up, dried and put back in the cupboards. I left the kitchen, intent on completing the next step in my plan, but Mother had other ideas.

"Mirabelle. In here. Now."

I walked into the room to see Mother smiling sweetly at me. Clarabelle was lying on the sofa fast asleep.

"Yes, Mother?" I said, hating that I still had to call her that, but still used to the feel of it on my tongue.

She stared above my head as she spoke. "Polish the room then clean the fridge. If you do a good job, I might let you eat with Little Doll and I tonight. Would you like that?"

"Yes, Mother."

"But if you miss just one spot..." she trailed off, her eyes glinting.

She picked up Clarabelle and kissed the top of the little girl's head tenderly. Clarabelle did not stir. She looked like Sleeping Beauty. *And I'm Cinderella.*

My kidnapper left the room with slow, mocking steps, holding the little girl close to her chest like she was the most precious thing in the world. I vaguely remembered how she used to hold me like that and felt a stabbing pain in my chest. There was no point dwelling on the past; I had to focus on the now - on getting Clarabelle and myself out of the dragon's lair unscathed.

Now that I knew what she had done, I realised there was no way to predict the full extent of her wrongness. Her badness. Would she harm me?

My eyes fell on the dining room table, to the empty syringe that Mother had boldly left out on display. I shouldn't have been shocked, but I was. I picked up the syringe and shook my head. Did she drug me too? And if Clarabelle was drugged, how was I supposed to get her out of the house. I could carry her, but not for long. I looked at my scrawny arms, at my bandaged hand. I wasn't exactly muscle girl.

I hurried to the cleaning cupboard under the stairs and grabbed a dust cloth and the polish spray. I placed them on the carpet behind me then knelt down and rummaged around inside the cupboard looking for a bag, one big enough to hold all of my supplies. I gritted my teeth, worried. There was nothing in the cupboard of any use. Nothing. I re-considered escaping without any supplies. Would I survive with nothing but the clothes on my back? I didn't even have any warm clothes, but the month was May, so it should not be too cold. The only shoes I possessed were a flimsy pair of slippers. My feet were much smaller than Mother's so there was little point in taking a pair of her outdoor boots. But the problem of starving to death was one I had to deal with. I had to find a bag to carry those food tins.

The distant banging sound that I had heard before made me jump. Mother came running down the stairs, face red and twisted with anger. I hastily picked up the polish and cloth as she ran past me into the kitchen. I heard the kitchen door being unlocked and hurried into the room to see her disappear out of the back door. What on earth was she doing? The kitchen door was ajar. Light ran down the gap, sucking me forward. It would be so easy to slip out of that door and make a run for it, but I couldn't leave Clarabelle.

I heard Mother screaming something incoherent and the banging sound stopped. Was someone out there? Who was she screaming at? I crept toward the door, desperate to know what was happening outside, but the sound of approaching footsteps made me dash back out of the room into the hallway.

She locked the kitchen door then whipped past me, saying, "After you've done your chores, go upstairs and take off that dress. I've laid out some other clothes for you. From now on, you're to wear those and only those."

My question died on my tongue. It would be stupid to ask her about what had just happened anyway. The less I engaged with her the better.

She disappeared upstairs and I began to polish the dining room table all the while puzzling over the bag issue. The trunks in the attic were far too large and bulky, so those were out. There were no bags in any of the other rooms in the cottage, except, maybe, in Mother's room. I remembered the large black holdall she had brought Clarabelle home in. That would be perfect. Of course, I was not allowed in her bedroom. I had never even stepped foot in it. But my kidnapper did not lock the room; she simply trusted me not to break her rules.

I smiled. The old me would never have dreamt of doing such a thing, but I wasn't the old me anymore. I was Polly Dalton.

Chapter Fifteen

My kidnapper left the house that afternoon leaving me free to sneak into her bedroom unnoticed. Clarabelle was as quiet as a mouse, fast asleep no doubt behind the locked door of the spare room. The cottage was quiet too, unnervingly so. Every step I took sounded like an elephant's.

I wore the plain, brown, sack-like dress Mother had left out on my bed. I had changed out of my doll dress into the brown one just before she left the cottage. Now I looked like the little slave girl I had recently become. The material of the dress – if you could call it a dress – was scratchy and coarse against my sensitive skin, and the fabric smelt musty. Despite the roughness of the dress, there was something wonderful about not having to wear one of my doll dresses, because that's what they were. They were dresses for dolls not human beings. Mother did not wear silly dresses like that; she wore jeans and jumpers and blouses.

She had just left the house dressed in pale blue flares and an orange and white striped blouse. I wondered where she was going, how long it would take her to reach the closest house or shop. I knew she had a car, because I heard the roll of its wheels on hard ground and the low growl of its engine whenever she left the cottage. If only I could drive, I could whisk Clarabelle – who I ought to start thinking of as Emma – and myself far away from this dark, dingy place with speed and ease. But Mother never mentioned her car. She had usually held back from talking about the outside. I used to think it was to spare my feelings, but now I knew the truth. Anger surged in my breast, giving me the courage to cross the landing to my kidnapper's bedroom. Forbidden territory. Under no circumstances was I allowed in that room.

Cursing my trembling hand, I turned the door knob and pushed. Immediately, the scent of orange-blossom filled my nostrils. I stared at what I could see with the door partially open: a huge pine wardrobe stood on the right side of the room. A pine bedside table stood beside a neatly made double bed whose sheets were pure white. The bed bathed in a glorious pool of yellow light.

I stepped into the room, squinting against its brightness: on the far side of the bedroom was an open window, a window that was not blacked out or boarded up. An open window that allowed beautiful, bright, sparkling, wondrous light to pour unfiltered into the room. My eyes burned and began to water, but my feet transported me, dream-like, to the shimmering window. I blinked furiously, willing my eyes to adjust and allow me to enjoy this heavenly sight, but they blurred and tears welled, blinding me. Still, my feet carried me on, past the bottom of the bed, towards the warmth of the glorious sunlight. I could hear birds chirping, smell fresh, clean, rich air which broke through the orange-blossom fragrance, beating it away until there was nothing left but the smell of fresh, sun-glossed air.

For a long time – how long I don't know – I stood in front of the open window, eyes shielded by my left hand, salty tears freely flowing down my pale cheeks, taking my fill of the outside. How dare she keep me from this. In that moment, I didn't care how traumatised she was. All I cared about was getting back the freedom she stole from me ten years ago.

I inhaled deeply and stared in wonder at the view that stretched so temptingly before my eyes: first there was a small front lawn, wild and overgrown with long grass so green it hurt my eyes almost as much as the sunlight. Through this tangle of grass weaved a stepping stone path, the stones of which were pale grey and made smaller by the encroaching blades of grass. The garden wilderness was closed in by a wooden fence that must have stood only as high as my waist and which looked broken and battered in places. Beyond the fence lay a dirt road on either side of which stood masses of tall, looming trees. In Mother's magazines and books - on the rare occasion she had shown me - I had seen these things: trees, grass, bushes, sun, sky, farms, houses, animals, but never had I seen them for real. So now I stared and stared, feasting on these sights, delighting in their realness.

The thicket of trees stretched on far into the distance, but beyond the dirt road I could see a proper road made of some kind of stone, and then, far away, a beautiful assortment of differently coloured fields which splayed out in all directions, one of which held grazing sheep that resembled little clumps of cotton wool. Beyond the sheep field lay a sea of houses which, from this distance, seemed large enough only to house dolls.

Clouds floated across the sun, giving me some relief. I lowered my arm and stared open-mouthed at the scenery. At those houses in the distance. Did my parents live in one of those houses? Eagerness and excitement snapped me into action. I turned away from the window and scanned my kidnapper's bedroom. There was nothing unusual at all about the room. The carpet was beige. The bedside table held nothing but a small lamp and a book entitled, 'Rosemary's Baby'. No pictures hung from the walls. A second wardrobe stood to my right, the door ajar just a touch, as if it was too full to close properly.

Aware that I had wasted precious time, I walked straight over to the wardrobe and pulled open both doors.

For a second I thought my mind was playing tricks on me. But as I continued to stare at the freak display lining the shelves of the wardrobe, my heartbeat quickened and my mouth grew dry.

The wardrobe was full of dolls. Every shelf was lined with dolls – some naked, some clothed. From the clothes rail hung more dolls all of which were tied to the metal pole by their hair. They dangled there lifelessly. There must have been at least fifty dolls crammed in there and though every single doll was different, they all had one thing in common: every single doll had a photograph taped over its face - a photograph of a young woman whose eyes had been coloured in with red ink. Some photographs had been coloured in so forcefully that holes had punctured the paper revealing the dead, beady doll eyes that lay beneath.

She was a sick, angry woman. I did not know her at all.

I stumbled away from the wardrobe and swivelled toward the open window as the unmistakable sound of a knock on the front door penetrated the cottage. Rushing toward the window, I grabbed the sill and peered out and down – a man stood down there. A man! A fully fledged other person! He wore a green T-shirt. His brown hair hung around his broad shoulders. A heavy-looking bag hung off his back. He knocked again and I hesitated, wanting to call out to him, but unsure whether to trust this stranger. What if he was as damaged as her?

My chance was stolen from me as Mother's red car grumbled up the dirt road. Unable to believe her timing, I dashed around the bottom of the bed, out of the room. Closing the door behind myself, I moved to the edge of the banister at the top of the stairs. I knelt down and peered around the corner giving myself a view of the front door. My heart raced as I realised this could be my chance – mine and Emma's chance - to escape. The man had looked bigger than Mother, stronger too. If he was a good, undamaged person, surely he would help us.

The 'if' word hovered over me like some invisible beast; what if he was even worse than her? What if she knew him? What if they were partners? I shook my head, unable to believe I could have been so utterly blind as to not pick up on her having some kind of evil ally in all of this. Surely I would have seen or noticed something.

I heard voices – hers and his. It was hard to hear their words and I wanted to know – I needed to know. I pushed myself up and ran down the stairs then darted past the front door into the living room where I hid just inside the doorway by the corner wall. I pressed my ear to the cool, hard outer wall and strained to hear their words, but they had stopped talking.

In all of my ten years at the cottage I could not remember a single time she had mentioned a man other than her grandfather who she had only so recently spoken to me about. Once, some years back, I had asked her who my father was. Somewhere deep down, even at six or seven years of age, I had known this was forbidden territory, but my inner cat had gotten the better of me. She had shouted at me for asking such a question then given me the silent treatment for the next seven days. Those seven days had seemed an eternity to me. I had begged her to talk to me, tried to hug her, brought her glasses of water, made her lunch, but to no avail.

I shivered, realising that she treated me like that because she enjoyed feeling powerful. She enjoyed tormenting me. If I did not get Emma out of the cottage, Mother would do the same to her – maybe worse if Emma was not as biddable as me. As weak and pathetic and gullible as me.

If she is not as weak as me, she'll probably suffer more.

I was weak. For ten long years, I had been weak. I had behaved like some kind of toy puppet on a string. Like a stupid, mindless doll – exactly what she wanted.

Well, not anymore.

My hands clenched at my sides and I set my jaw, determined to take advantage of this opportunity.

The lock crunched, the front door opened and I stepped out of my hiding place into full view.

Chapter Sixteen

"Come in, come in. I'm sure you'll feel much better once you've had something to eat and drink," Mother said. Her voice was high and happy-sounding. Unnaturally buoyant, I thought.

My first thought was why – why was she inviting the man inside? She was acting like she had nothing to hide.

She paused just inside the front door, holding the door half-open, and started when she saw me. "Get back upstairs into your room this instant," she hissed, her eyes shooting daggers.

I stared back at her and shook my head. "No. I'm not going anywhere." I couldn't believe my boldness. I had never answered back. Never. My heartbeat rocketed but I planted my feet, determined to stay.

Shock pulled at her features. She stabbed her finger at me. "If you don't get upstairs now, you'll pay for it," she hissed.

I said nothing, only watched in silence, my eyes greedy with curiosity as the man's face poked through the gap in the door.

"Everything alright, Miss?" he said. He had a strange lilt to his accent and he pronounced 'th' as 't' which made me think he might be from another country.

She laughed and beckoned him inside, moving into the hallway. "Yes, everything's fine. Come on in. This is my daughter. Don't mind her."

She stood beside the door and held it open for him then closed and locked it. She slid the keys into her pocket. The man raised his eyebrows at her for locking the door. She smiled and shrugged.

"You can't be too careful living out here in the middle of nowhere," she said with a girly laugh.

He nodded then looked at me. I saw him take in my odd, potato-sack dress. A flicker of confusion flashed up in his dark brown eyes. He gave me a small, awkward smile. I stared back, taking all of him in, trying to work out who he was. He had a symmetrical, good-looking face and a square jaw. His forehead was shiny with sweat. He did not have any wrinkles around his eyes like her, which meant he was younger. How much younger, I couldn't be sure. He looked fine – on the outside.

The young man looked from me to Mother's retreating back. She was heading toward the kitchen, walking in a weird way, her hips swaying from side to side like the pendulum in the grandfather clock.

She was almost out of earshot, but I couldn't be sure. How could I know he was trustworthy? He could be thinking anything right now. Behind those tired, innocent-seeming brown eyes, he could be thinking cruel, evil, wicked thoughts. That was the horrifying truth; no-one could know what someone else was thinking. Thoughts were private. There was no need to make an effort to hide them even, because they remained as silent as the dead, voiced only in your own head; right now, she did not have a clue that I was thinking about whether to ask this man for help or not, just as I had no clue what he was thinking or what Mother was thinking. The fact terrified me. I stared at the back of his head as he turned away from me with a puzzled look on his face. He followed her into the kitchen with slow, weary steps, his bag still weighing heavily on his back.

I followed him, heart thumping, unable to make a decision. To trust or not to trust?

He paused at the kitchen doorway. "Why're the windows like that?"

"Come in, come in. Take off that heavy bag and rest yourself," she said, bustling about the kitchen humming 'Dancing Queen'.

"The windows?" he repeated with a yawn, still standing.

My kidnapper turned to face him. I noticed her top two buttons were undone exposing the top of her breasts. She smiled, "Oh that? That's because my poor little Mirabelle here is allergic to sunlight. Such a shame, but it can't be helped. Poor little thing. Now, what would you prefer, Patrick, ham or cheese sandwiches?"

Her words sounded so false. They were so false. She was false. Everything about her was pretend.

Anger pulsed through my veins and I opened my mouth to say that she was lying, that she had kidnapped me, that she had taken Emma too, but the words melted away as the young man made sympathetic noises, glanced pityingly at me, then dropped his bag to the floor and took a seat at the table, a huge sigh whooshing out of him.

I hovered in the doorway staring at the back of Patrick's head, indecision coursing through me. Patrick. Such a simple, nice name. Could someone called Patrick who looked so normal on the outside be secretly damaged and evil on the inside?

Mother handed him a glass of water which he glugged back noisily. Without warning, she turned to me and said brightly, "Off you go now, darling, up to bed for your afternoon rest."

She walked over and seized my wrist in a painfully tight grip. She dragged me out of the room glaring down at me, a warning clear in her small dark eyes. I did not fight back, though I longed to. She shut the kitchen door in my face and I stood there, small and pathetic in the shadows, battling the urge to cry.

Laughter – his and hers – erupted from behind the door, making my tummy hurt.

I heard a noise coming from above and strained to listen. It was Emma and she was crying. I tensed, fearful that Mother would hear. I glanced from the kitchen door to the ceiling, stuck again. Should I go to Emma and calm her down or should I burst into the kitchen, tell Patrick everything? There was no telling what Mother would do, how she would react. A small part of me still felt bad for even considering the idea of telling someone what she had done – what she was still doing. It felt like some kind of betrayal, which was ridiculous, because it was her who had betrayed me. She was the one who had stolen me from my parents when I was only three years old. I knew I had to pull myself together. She was dangerous. I had to get Emma and myself out of there. I had to get home, back to my real parents where I would be safe, but there was no telling how trustworthy this young man was. He had turned up uninvited on Mother's doorstep with nothing but a big bag on his back. Who did that? Why would someone be wondering around in these woods alone? Was he running from someone? Was he a criminal running from the police? If he was, there was no way I could place my trust in him, not when there was so much at stake.

Rack my brains as I might, I could not come up with a rational explanation for this man's solitary presence in the woods or his sudden arrival at the cottage. It didn't make any sense. I ran through his actions in my mind. He had sat down with obvious relief, as if exhausted. He had gulped that glass of water down so quickly...but why would someone be wandering alone in the middle of nowhere? It seemed absurd. Was he a homeless man searching for a home? Maybe. That was the first idea that made some sort of sense. But then – why was he homeless in the first place? Had he done something bad that had made him lose his home? It was impossible to know.

Emma's crying escalated to screams. The kitchen went quiet. The door opened and I stepped back as my kidnapper froze at the sight of me standing there.

I thought it was only wolves that snarled – like in 'Beauty and the Beast' and 'The Wolves of Willoughby Chase' - but right then, she snarled at me, bearing her small, sharp teeth and yellow-pink gums, her lips curled back, her nose scrunched up. Her eyes looked black in the gloom of the hallway and her body towered over me like a skeletal giant. Her blouse hung loose revealing the ribs between her small breasts. She was so thin, unhealthily so, and I wondered if she had lost weight recently.

I stumbled backward, sure she was going to hit me, but something changed in her eyes. Her expression softened and she relaxed her face. I could almost see the cogs whirring in her brain as she changed her plan of attack.

"Go upstairs and calm Clarabelle down, please, little doll. I'm busy entertaining our guest." Her voice was soft – and completely false.

I glanced down at her hands, which were balled into fists beside her skinny thighs.

I hesitated, knowing I was taking a risk. She glanced back over her shoulder, her brow creased.

"I'll need the key," I said quietly.

"The key?" she said, genuinely confused.

"The key to her room," I said, determined not to call Emma by her fake name, "I can only calm her down properly if I can see her, give her a cuddle."

The scrape of a chair from the kitchen and Patrick's voice, asking if everything was okay, seemed to force her into a decision.

"Everything's fine – back in a second!" she called, her voice high and girly again.

She pulled out the key ring from her pocket and hastily removed the spare room key. I noticed her fingers were trembling. The old me would have asked if she was alright, but I wasn't Mirabelle the weak anymore.

"Thank you, Mother," I said softly.

Then, before she could change her mind, I turned and walked back up the hallway. She went back into the kitchen and shut the door as I ran up the stairs, taking them two at a time, my heart about to burst with excitement and nerves. This was it. This was the first real step.

I knocked on the door. "Hi," I said gently, "It's only me."

Emma stopped wailing. I unlocked the door and slipped into the room, clutching the key tightly in my sweaty palm, so tightly it made my hand throb.

The little girl sat on the bed hugging her knees to her chest. Her eyes were red and swollen from crying. Snot ran from her nose onto her lips. I looked around the room, relieved to find it as normal as mine though more colourful as the walls had been painted pale pink and a fluffy white rug lay on the wooden floorboards. Mother had made more of an effort this time. From the windows hung bright pink curtains which had been nailed around the edges into the wall. The middle of the curtains had been sown together to prevent even the slightest shard of light from penetrating the room.

"Hi," I said, perching on the edge of the bed.

She stared at me with her big blue eyes and sniffed. "My head hurts."

"Does it? Oh, well, maybe if we go downstairs I can find something to make it feel better."

"I'm not allowed," she whispered, her eyes darting toward the door, "M, M, Mother will be cross if, if, if I go out."

"No she won't. She sent me up here to see if you were okay, but there's something important I have to tell you first. A secret."

Emma sat up at this. I noticed she wore one of my old nightgowns. A long white one embroidered with daisies. A strange twinge pulled at my chest. She was my replacement.

I leaned forward and stroked her hair out of her eyes.

"What secret?" she said.

"If I tell you, you have to promise me not to say anything. Promise?"

She hesitated, looked at the door again. After a few seconds she whispered, "I promise."

"Okay," I paused, trying to think of the best way to explain, "the woman who is looking after us isn't well. There's something wrong with her. She took me from my real parents when I was about your age and told me I was her daughter. She told me my name was Mirabelle, but my real name is Polly. And now she's doing the same thing to you."

"I don't understand," Emma said, wiping her nose with the back of her wrist.

"What's your name? Your *real* name?"

The girl frowned, as if concentrating really hard. She had been here for only a month or so. There was no way she could have forgotten her real name already, but Mother was clever. She skewed the truth, made you think the way she thought.

"My old name is Emma," she whispered.

"Yes! That's right. Emma is your *real* name. Polly is mine. She stole us from our real parents. She took us because she wanted us, but we have to get away. We have to get out of here and go back to our real parents."

Emma stared at me. I could see that she was trying to wrap her brain around my meaning. But then she shook her head, "No. She's nice to me. She loves me. She's my mummy now. She said, she said, that, that..."

"She *lied*. She's not your mummy. She took you away, Emma, don't you see? We have to get away from here."

"But, but, but, I can't. I can't go outside. The light will, will, will...hurt me."

I shook my head and took her hands in mine. They were so small, so innocent.

"The light won't hurt you. She lies. It's all lies."

"Grownups don't tell lies," Emma said firmly.

I sighed. How was I going to get her to believe me? She had to trust me or everything could go wrong.

"Your real mummy and daddy don't tell lies. Most grownups don't, but she does. She's different."

"Why?"

"Why what?"

"Why does she lie?"

I shrugged and tucked her hair behind her ear. "I don't know. I wish I did, but I don't. All I know is that we need to get out of here, away from her. We need to go and find our real parents."

"I'm scared," she said.

"You don't need to be scared. You just need to do everything I tell you to. Okay?"

She nodded, but her eyes wandered to the door.

"Promise me you'll do what I say, when I say it? Emma, promise me."

She looked at me, her eyes wide and wet, "I promise."

"Good. Good girl. Okay. This is what we're going to do."

Chapter Seventeen

"Mother! Mother! Come quick! It's Clarabelle!" I screamed the words at the top of my lungs, standing just outside the spare room. I screamed the words over and over and over, only stopping when Mother's footsteps pounded up the stairs. She turned sharply on the landing, using the banister to propel her round.

"What happened? What have you done to her?" she screamed, eyes crazed, full of panic.

"I don't know! She's in bed and she won't move!" I panted back. I pointed through the open doorway to the bed. An Emma-sized mound lay beneath the bed covers.

"Move!" she barked at me, rushing into the room, "Clarabelle! Clarabelle, talk to me!"

The second she was fully inside the room, I slammed the door shut and frantically jammed the key into the lock. She was back at the door immediately, the ruse blown, twisting and turning the door knob, screaming and cursing - but the job was already done. I had locked the door. She was trapped. Her fists continued to pound against the door. I stumbled backwards and turned around, unable to believe what I'd just done yet able to keep moving.

"Come on!" I yelled at Emma, who poked her terrified face out of my bedroom door, shaking her head.

"I don't want to!" she cried.

I grabbed her hand. "You have to. Remember your promise?"

She hesitated then nodded and I tugged her out of my bedroom, across the landing to the stairs. Mother's screams were crazed, her rage terrifying. Her fists pounded and bashed the door with so much force I feared she was going to break it down.

"Run!" I shouted, pulling Emma down the stairs.

We reached the second last step and stopped. Patrick stood at the bottom of the stairs looking concerned. In that moment, he looked huge and almost as terrifying as Mother.

"Hey, hey, hey! Slow down girls. What's going on?" he said, holding up his hands.

I sucked in a quick breath, knowing I had to get this right, hoping he was a good person. "Please help us. She's not our -"

Mother's voice cut across mine, drowning me out, "DON'T LET THEM OUTSIDE, PATRICK! THEY'RE ALLERGIC TO THE LIGHT! THEY'LL DIE!"

Patrick sighed. "Girls, what's going on?" He crouched down at the foot of the stairs and smiled sympathetically.

I pulled Emma close to my side and tried to sound as mature and clear as I could. "You have to find a way to get us out of here. We need to leave. She's not our real mother. She's-"

"Now, now, slow down there girl. You're scaring your little sis." He reached out to pat my arm but I jerked back out of his reach. His eyebrows shot upwards and he chuckled and shook his head.

"Look, I get it. You have this horrid, rare disorder and it must be mad awful having to stay cooped up inside here all the time, but it's not your mother's fault. She has to keep you inside. It's her job to protect you."

I shook my head and tried to stay calm, tried to ignore Mother's ranting from above us. "Please, you have to believe me. She's *not* our mother. She took me from my parents ten years ago. My real name's Polly Dalton. And she took Emma from her parents just one month ago. Surely you heard about a missing girl? It must have been in the newspaper."

He looked like he hadn't heard me. His eyes were on the ceiling, his attention on Mother's words, not mine.

I grabbed his arm and tugged. "Please, Patrick, please. You have to help us. The front door and the back door are locked. All of the downstairs windows are nailed shut, but maybe..."

"I'm not from around here," he said, looking at my hand on his arm, "so I don't know about any story like the one you're talking about, but I have to say, it all sounds pretty far-fetched, you know?"

I let my hand drop to my side. "Emma, you tell him. Tell the nice man what happened to you."

I looked down at Emma whose face was buried in my side. Crouching down beside her, I whispered reassuring things and stroked her back, but she burst into inconsolable tears.

"I wa, wa, wa, want, my, mu, mu, mummy!" she wailed.

Mother heard Emma and shouted, "Don't worry, little doll, mummy's right here!"

I gritted my teeth and stood up. "Patrick, please, I know it sounds strange – and it is – believe me, I know how strange it sounds. I believed she was my mother until only a few days ago, but I'm telling you the truth. She's crazy. She may seem normal, but she's not. She's insane. She kidnapped me and she kidnapped Emma."

Tears of desperation streamed down my cheeks. "Please, Patrick, I'm begging you. Please believe me."

His face creased with concern. "Has she hurt you? Does she...hit you?"

"No, but, but I want to go home, back to my real parents. I shouldn't be here. Emma shouldn't be here. It's not right."

Patrick began to nod. He tugged on his earlobe. A frown had etched itself into his forehead making him look older. Finally, he sighed and looked me dead in the eye.

"Okay. I've heard you. I'm not saying I believe you completely, but it does seem like one helluva a big lie for such a little girl to make up...but I'm not about to go around smashing windows or dismantling them. For all I know, you being cooped up in here could have made you so desperate to get outside that you don't care anymore about being allergic to light."

I opened my mouth to speak but he held up his hands. "Hang on, hang on. What I'm saying is, I'm going to go upstairs and talk to your mother."

"She isn't-"

"Okay, okay – she isn't your mother – I get that. So I'm going to talk to her, get her side of things then I'll see about what's best."

I shook my head. "No. Please don't let her talk to you. Please just help us get out of here. You could leave right now. Go to the closest town and get the police. Bring them here. They'll know. They'll sort it all out then you don't have to do anything wrong."

He frowned. "Yeah, but you're forgetting one little itty bitty thing: the doors are locked and she's got the keys. How am I going to get out without breaking something?"

The question dangled in the air like a poised blade; he was right.

I swallowed thickly. "Good point. Alright then, but before you talk to her, please can you just wait a second. There's something in the attic that will prove what I'm saying is true. Please? Is that okay? It'll only take me five minutes."

He sighed. Mother had gone silent. He shifted his weight from one foot to the other, tugging on his earlobe. "Okay. But be quick. She's gone quiet and it's worrying me."

"Thank you, Patrick. Thank you so much."

I extricated Emma from my side and told her to sit on the stairs and wait for me. She resisted a little, but after a few reassuring words she gave in and sank to the carpet with a sob.

Patrick followed me up the stairs. I raced up, taking them two at a time, aware that I had to be quick or he might change his mind.

Standing on my desk chair, I opened the attic door then pulled out the ladder. Patrick helped me lower it to the ground then held it firm as I ascended quickly, my heart thumping against my ribs. I reached the opening to the attic and heard Mother's voice, urgent and low, directed at Patrick. She must have heard us climbing the stairs. I thought about turning round and telling Patrick to ignore her, but knew she would just keep talking and he would feel compelled to listen, so I pushed myself to my feet quickly and scanned the boxes. With a horrible moment of clarity, I remembered: I had tucked the evidence inside my pillowcase! The newspaper article wasn't up here in the attic; it was down there in my bedroom.

Cursing my forgetfulness, I clambered back down the ladder to hear K urging Patrick to get the key to the spare room off me and let her out. Patrick glanced from me to the spare room, clearly torn. Before he could decide what to do, I jumped off the ladder and ran into my bedroom. I shoved my hand into the pillowcase, terrified that she had somehow found and taken my evidence. My hand found nothing, nothing but pillow and cotton, and then – paper – the article. With sweaty fingers, I pulled out the piece of newspaper. Patrick had to believe me now. He *had* to. The resemblance between the now-me and my three year old self was undeniable. I had barely changed. My face was thinner and I was obviously a lot taller; yet my big, almond-shaped eyes were exactly the same. That girl was me. I was that girl.

"Patrick! I found it! Look!" I ran out of my room onto the landing.

Patrick was standing close to the spare room door, his ear pressed against the wood. He was nodding, tugging his earlobe, frowning.

"Patrick?" I said, walking toward him.

He turned slowly. His face looked different, harder somehow. I took a step back, suddenly worried. What had she said to him? Had she convinced him not to trust me?

"Patrick, please, just have a look…"

"Where's the key?" he said, "She's having an asthma attack. You have to let her out now."

"She doesn't have asthma," I said, thrusting the newspaper article forward, "Please, just look. This is proof. If you don't believe me after looking at this, I'll give you the key. I promise."

"Help…me," Mother's voice floated through the door.

"She's lying," I said quickly as his head jerked toward her voice.

He sighed and snatched the paper out of my hand. "What am I supposed to be looking at exactly?"

I said nothing, just watched as he focused on the picture of me. His eyebrows rose a fraction and he glanced at me then back at the black and white photograph, at me then back at the article again. His eyes darted side to side as he read the article. A few moments later, his back straightened and his eyes widened. He slipped the article into his pocket and glanced back at the spare room. He put his finger to his lips and pointed to the stairs.

Relief exploded in my chest - he understood! He was on my side. Our side. Mine and Emma's. We were going to get out of here.

I wanted to scream with joy but I kept quiet and followed him down the stairs to where Emma still sat, hugging her knees. I tapped her shoulder and put my finger to my lips. Patrick beckoned us to follow him into the kitchen and we did, hand in hand, Emma looking curiously up at me through wet, swollen eyes.

Once we were in the kitchen, Patrick said, "I can't believe it – it all seems so far out - but that *is* you. You're her. The girl from the paper. The one who went missing all those years ago."

I nodded, waited for him to take charge.

He cleared his throat. "Is there a spare key anywhere? For the front or the back door?"

"I don't know," I said.

"Let's have a quick look. If we can find a spare key, it'll be a helluva a lot easier to get out of here, and she's not going anywhere, crazy bitch – excuse my French."

"I'll look upstairs in her bedroom. You two look down here," I said eagerly.

He began opening the kitchen doors, directing Emma to look in the dining room for a key. I ran upstairs, making my steps as light as possible and entered Mother's bedroom, pausing outside the spare room, surprised to hear nothing. I wondered briefly what she was up to then refocused on the task at hand: finding a spare key.

I hunted high and low in both wardrobes – the normal one and the crazy, doll-filled one. Nothing. The bedside table drawer yielded nothing. I looked under the bed and under her pillows, inside her pillowcases. Nothing.

Sighing heavily, I went back downstairs to find Patrick checking the back of the framed photograph of Mother and her grandfather. He shook his head when he saw me.

"Looks like I'm going to have to get these boards off the windows. Do you know where she keeps her tools?"

"Cupboard under the stairs, I think."

He headed out of the room and Emma and I followed him. This was it. We were getting out of here. I began to relax. Patrick was an adult. He was going to get us out of here. I smiled at Emma and gave her a hug.

"Patrick's going to help us get out now. We're going home!"

She gave me a small smile and hugged me back. We watched as Patrick charged back into the living room with a screwdriver in his hand.

"Can I do anything to help?" I said, pulling Emma into the room.

He shook his head. Sweat had beaded on his brow. His fingers shook and he looked pale.

"Patrick, are you okay?" I said.

"Yep. Just hungry."

Needing something to do, I dashed into the kitchen and grabbed a piece of ham out of the fridge. I left the kitchen and hurried back into the living room. Patrick had managed to unscrew two nails so far. Emma sat on the floor cross-legged watching him, rocking back and forth, sucking her nightgown. I handed him the ham and he gobbled it down with unbelievable speed; I don't think he even chewed it.

There were only fifteen more screws to go. I tried to stand still but I couldn't. My legs wanted to move. I moved to stand behind Emma and stroked her hair in an effort to sooth her.

"Everything's going to be okay, Emma," I said, "You'll be able to see your mummy very soon."

As I said this, excitement stirred in my chest. I was going home. I was going to get away from here. Get to see the outside.

Twelve more screws to go and I'd be free.

I began to smile but my face froze; Patrick, Emma and I turned in the direction of the front door at the sound of it being unlocked. Before any of us could move, K slammed the door shut and locked it. She pocketed the key and turned to face us with a triumphant smile on her face.

Chapter Eighteen

Blood poured from her knees soaking through the denim of her jeans. Strands of short blonde hair clung like yellow spiders' legs to her sweaty cheeks and her hands were grazed. She smiled but the smile did not meet her eyes, which were wider than normal and distant, like they were not quite in this moment, or even like they were not quite human. Those wide, crazed eyes burned into mine and I tool an involuntary step back just as Patrick stepped in front of me and Emma, his arms relaxed by his sides, the screwdriver left on the edge of the window sill. He was only an inch or so taller than Mother, but far broader, far stronger. If it came to it – which I desperately hoped it wouldn't – he would beat her in a fight.

The silence stretched on, infinite and strangely deafening. I thought about speaking, just to break the tension, but I couldn't find the right words. Words seemed to have shrivelled up and rolled deep down into the fuzzy dark part of my mind. Emma's hand slipped into mine and I drew her close, stroking her hair. I wanted to whisper something reassuring to her but again words ran from me, spiralling down, down, down...

It was Patrick who finally spoke. "Let's all just calm down and talk, shall we?"

Mother's eyes shifted from mine to his, remaining oddly wide. She tilted her head to the side and smiled sweetly, smoothing down her wild hair. "What's there to talk about? Mirabelle played a silly little prank because she was trying to show off and everything's just gotten out of hand. Why don't I go and cook us a lovely roast dinner, crackling and all?"

"My name's not Mirabelle," I said, trying to keep the wobble out of my voice, "It's Polly. Polly Dalton."

Mother's whole body jerked as if she'd been shot. Somehow her false smile stayed on her face; she didn't even look at me. She took a small step toward Patrick. "See, Patrick, she's not well. She's very, very confused. It's not her fault and I try to be patient, but sometimes it really gets to me. She has these strange ideas – did she tell you I'm not her mother? Did she tell you that I kidnapped her? She's very muddled up, bless her, and I know I shouldn't lose my temper and get so angry, but I'm only human and dealing with her on my own has been hard. So hard, really.

"Poor little dot was diagnosed with light allergy disorder when she was just three years old. The doctors couldn't explain what caused it or how it came along. I cried for I don't know how many days. I didn't know what to do – Mirabelle's father, bless his soul, died when she was only two so that left just me on my own to cope with it all. Luckily, my grandfather left this cottage to me along with enough money to keep us going without me having to work, so I've home-schooled Mirabelle ever since. She's such a brave, resilient child, and it shouldn't come as a surprise that not being able to go outside has finally got to her, but, as you can see, it clearly has..."

Her eyes shifted to mine, the fire and anger gone in an instant. Now she was all love and warmth and kindness. "Mirabelle, sweetheart, I'm sorry I lost my temper. Please forgive me, and I should not have focused so much on Clarabelle these past weeks. I know you've been confused and maybe even a little jealous, but everything's going to go back to how it was, okay, little doll?"

I didn't say anything. I was too angry to speak. I glared at her, unable to say all that I wanted to, unable to correct her lies.

Patrick put his hand in his pocket and pulled out the newspaper article. With slow hands, he unfolded and smoothed out the paper.

"How do you explain this?" he said, thrusting the paper toward her.

She frowned as if confused and stepped forward to get a closer look at my evidence. A moment passed and another and another. Her head was bowed over the article so I couldn't see her face. I wondered what she was thinking; she must know her lies were blown; she must know Patrick would never believe her now. I tried to predict what she would do now that she knew it was impossible to get Patrick on her side, but she was hard to predict. I had never been able to put myself in her shoes and think forward to her next move. Never. Again I found myself stuck in uncertainty.

Patrick glanced round at me and gave me a reassuring smile. I nodded back and pulled Emma even closer. We were getting out of here soon. I just had to be patient.

Mother looked up, eyes wide with surprise. "Why that was my friend's little girl who went missing all those years ago. She was the pure image of Mirabelle, so I can see why, in her distress and confusion, poor Mirabelle thinks that's her," she looked back at me, her eyes welling up with tears, her face crumpling with misery, "Is that why you've been staying away from me the last few days, little doll? You poor little thing – you thought that I..." she trailed off, her wet eyes searching Patrick's.

"What about Emma?" Patrick said, although he sounded less certain of himself now.

"Emma?" she said, clearly confused.

At last, I found my words. Rage and fear burst out of me in one hot flow, "You kidnapped me! You kidnapped Emma! You're lying now! You're insane. Anyone can take one look at that photograph and know it's me!"

Patrick withdrew his outstretched arm. I could tell he was examining the article. Horror crept up my spine – was he doubting it?

Mother shook her hand and lowered her voice making it sound soft and soothing, "Mirabelle, sweetie, calm down. This isn't doing your health any good. Come with me and I'll tuck you up in bed."

I stepped forward and grabbed Patrick's arm. "Surely you don't believe her? Patrick? Please -"

"Ask Clarabelle," Mother said quietly.

Patrick looked down at me and shifted his weight. His fingers found his earlobe – a habit that I suddenly found the most irritating thing on earth. He shook his head, "I'm sorry, but..."

"No!" I shouted, "No! She's lying! She's crazy! I can show you – in her bedroom there's..."

"I'm happy to show you my bedroom, if you like Patrick. I simply want to put all of this to rest," she said, backing out of the room, "Follow me."

Patrick turned away from me and followed her out of the room. I let go of Emma and dashed past him, unable to believe Patrick's stupidity, yet following Mother closely, desperate to stop her from somehow hiding the evidence. It occurred to me that she may have a key for the doll wardrobe. She might run into the room and lock the wardrobe before anyone saw, then claim she'd lost the key or...Mother stopped outside her bedroom door and waved me and Patrick inside.

"Feel free to look around. I don't know what Mirabelle's talking about, but please feel free to look – just don't touch!" she added with a light chuckle.

I rushed past her into the room. Patrick followed me. I flung open the wardrobe doors and stood back, "See!"

"What the he-" Patrick's words stopped abruptly. Out of the corner of my eye I saw him fall, heard him gasp. Blood sprayed all over the bed, the walls, the carpet, me. Patrick fell onto his front on the carpet with a thud. He moaned, one hand on his bleeding side and swivelled to face Mother, his eyes wide with terror, his other hand held up in self-defence.

"Please, don't," he gasped. His eyes pleaded with her as she stood over him, a kitchen knife wet with his blood, her head tilted, eyes narrow.

She had *stabbed* him. I looked from the knife to her face, from her face to Patrick lying on the floor. It had all happened so fast. I blinked, trying to make it unso, but it happened. Mother had a knife and she had used it on Patrick. I couldn't move. My mouth was dry, my stomach like lead.

Mother stared down at Patrick, her eyes bright. "This would never have happened if you had read the sign - *Private Land* – it says it loud and clear. No-one else has ever come here. It's your own bloody fault for being such an ignorant fool," she spat, "If you'd just left well alone, this would never have happened."

Patrick's face crumpled. Tears leaked from the corners of his eyes. He squeezed his eyes shut and groaned.

"He's going to die. We have to help him," I said in a small, weak voice, eyeing the knife in her hand, too aware that it had sliced through Patrick's skin like butter only moments ago.

"And *you*," she said, turning to face me, jabbing the knife in my direction, "*you* disobeyed me, Mirabelle, didn't you? *You* went into the attic when I was out, didn't you? DIDN'T YOU!"

I stared at her, unable to believe I had been blind to her madness for so long.

"Answer me," she said.

I took a deep breath, "Yes. I went into the attic."

"Why?" She almost sounded hurt.

"I wanted to know more about your sister, but I found the newspaper article. I didn't want to believe it at first, but..." I trailed off as she switched her focus to Patrick, apparently bored of me.

"You're spoiling my lovely carpet," she said, narrowing her eyes, "Mirabelle, grab his legs. Help me carry him downstairs. Now."

"But-"

"*Now*, or..." she flicked her head at the knife in her hand, and I believed her. I believed she would hurt me too, or worse, if I refused to cooperate. I was no longer her little doll, the biddable, perfect, blue-eyed puppet who had to remain flawless. In her eyes, I was no longer a little girl. I was developing into a woman, which meant I was tainted; what did it matter now if I got a bruise or a cut? There was no need for me to be the image of perfection anymore; she had Emma.

Heart pounding, I moved to crouch behind Patrick whose face had gone sickly white. I gently lifted his hand away from his wound and picked up his other wrist, surprised to find his skin cold.

"Three, two, one!" Mother said and we heaved and lifted him up.

He groaned as blood oozed from the slice in his side. His face contorted with pain and he bit his lip as we half-dragged, half-carried him out of the room, across the landing and down the stairs, stopping every two steps to get our breath.

"You're heavier than you look," she said with a strange smile.

Emma appeared in the hallway chewing her nightgown. Mother snapped at her to go up to my bedroom and stay there.

"It's okay, Emma," I murmured, my eyes following her as she slipped past me and ran up the stairs.

"What are you going to do?" I said.

We had carried Patrick into the kitchen leaving a trail of thick, gooey blood in our wake. Patrick looked like death warmed up. He was losing too much blood. The metallic scent of blood drifted around the kitchen. Mother placed the knife on the counter and told me to sit down. I did as she said, though I perched on the edge of the chair, ready to move if a chance arose. She leant against the counter watching Patrick, her head tilted to the side, eyes glazed, her expression almost bored. A zigzag of dried blood smeared her right cheek and her nostrils flared as she struggled to regain her breath. Her tongue flicked out of her mouth to wet her thin, dry lips.

Chapter Nineteen

"What are you going to do now?" I repeated.

"This mess is *sickening*," she said, ignoring my question, her voice raw with spite, "Clean it up."

She grabbed the dishcloth and threw it at me. It hit me in the face. I hesitated. She glared, snapping at me to fetch the bucket from under the stairs.

I hurried away, slipping on Patrick's blood. I fell onto one knee and she tutted. Ignoring her, I left the kitchen and opened the cupboard under the stairs. My eyes found the bucket immediately. I grabbed it, pausing at the sight of Mother's tool box. There were no pockets in my dress, nowhere I could conceal anything. The spare room key was in my knickers, but there was no way of concealing anything larger like a hammer.

"Hurry up!"

I snatched up a small screwdriver and put it in the bucket. If she saw it I was done for, so I rushed into the kitchen, passing her as quickly as possible. With shaky hands I lifted the bucket into the sink and ran the hot tap.

"Add bleach," she said.

Obediently, I bent down and opened the cupboard under the sink, picked up the bleach and added a tiny amount to the hot water.

"More than that," she snapped.

I added two more drops and looked at her. She nodded sharply telling me to add more. I added more and more until she held up her hand to indicate that I should stop. Within seconds the harsh odour of bleach permeated the small room overwhelming the metallic zing of blood and making my nostrils burn. I gazed into the now steaming water, realising that if I was to plunge my hand into the liquid to retrieve the screwdriver, I would burn my skin. I glanced at Patrick as I turned off the tap. His body was utterly limp, his face ashen. Was he dead? It was impossible to tell in one quick glance. I glanced at Mother who stood gazing down at Patrick's body, leaning against the counter, her fingers only inches from the knife.

Hoping she would not notice, I turned on the cold tap and watched the water gush in, cooling off the steam.

"Not too cold," she said, whipping her head round to glare at me.

I turned off the cold tap and, with difficulty, lifted the bucket out of the sink onto the bloodied tiles.

"Can I have some gloves please, Mother?" I said.

She seemed not to hear me, so I stood up, opened the cupboard and rifled inside.

"No. No gloves. Hurry up."

Gritting my teeth, I got back down on my hands and knees and dipped the dishcloth into the top of the water in an attempt to keep my fingers dry. I could feel her watching me as I crawled toward a small droplet of blood to her right nearer the back door. The blood was still wet and I was able to wipe it up in one swipe. I crawled back to the bucket and rinsed the cloth, again conscious of keeping my fingers out of the water. With only two thirds of the cloth wet, I moved to the second furthest droplet of blood and began to clean it, my hands trembling, my fingers beginning to tingle as bleach made contact with my skin despite my efforts.

There were no more small droplets. My mouth went watery. I dipped the dish cloth into the bucket for a third time, keeping the part I was holding as dry as possible. I turned with the dish cloth raised and stared at the huge black-red puddle of blood beside Patrick, fighting a sudden surge of pointlessness. I stared at his chest. If he was dead, what was the point in trying to fight her now? I should wait for a better opportunity...a moment when I wasn't crawling around on my hands and knees with her standing over me and a knife close to hand.

"Do it," she snapped.

I inched toward the puddle, my eyes fixed on Patrick, on his face and chest, on the slightest hint of movement. *Breathe. Breathe. Please breathe.*

There! There it was! His chest – rising and falling – minutely – just enough!

In that instant, I plunged the whole cloth into the thick puddle of blood.

"Good girl. That's it," she said, almost breathless.

I fought the urge to throw up and focused on letting the cloth absorb as much of the blood as possible. It took only seconds for the cloth to become heavy with blood.

"I can't! I can't!" I cried, glancing over my shoulder at her, begging with my eyes.

Mother's eyes revealed only excitement. "Do it," she said.

I shook my head, "No. I'm going to be sick."

She stepped toward me, finger jabbing, "You *will* do it or I will make Clarabelle do it. Is that what you want?"

I shook my head and whispered something.

"What did you say?" she snapped, coming closer.

"Nothing," I murmured.

"Tell me!" she demanded.

"No!" I screamed, staring at the cloth in my hand.

She froze, shocked by my defiance, and I span around and thrust the blood-soaked cloth into her face. She screamed and clawed at the sodden cloth. At the same time, I plunged my hand into the bucket, barely feeling the burn, my fingers scrabbling for the screwdriver, but she was there, grabbing my hair, yanking me back, throwing me down on top of Patrick. I rolled off him onto my side and turned to face her. She reached down with both hands to grab my legs and I kicked and pushed myself up and stabbed the screwdriver into her thigh. She screeched and stumbled, falling into the counter, her hand scrabbling for the knife, eyes aflame, but she knocked the knife sending it spinning onto the floor under the fridge.

She fought to stand but fell, grabbing her thigh, screaming and cursing.

I darted to the counter, opened a drawer and pulled out a knife. "Keys," I said, pointing the knife down at her, careful to keep my distance.

Tears poured from her eyes. "I'm so sorry little doll. Please, please don't do this! If you go outside, you'll die - I love you - I never wanted any of this to happen!"

"Keys," I said.

She continued to sob and wail, clutching her injured thigh.

"*Keys.*"

She looked up at me and I could see her noting my determination, seeing how strong I was for the first time. With a shaking hand, she pulled the keys out of her pocket and tossed them weakly onto the floor.

"You'll die," she said weakly, closing her eyes and sobbing into her chest, "Clarabelle too. You'll both die."

"Don't move," I said, backing up to stand behind Patrick. Placing the knife on the floor beside me, never taking my eyes off her, I dragged Patrick out of the room into the hallway.

"Stay where you are!" I shouted, darting back into the room and picking up the knife, relieved to see she was still lying in a heap on the floor sobbing into her chest.

I backed out of the room slowly, the knife pointed in her direction. "Goodbye *Mother.*"

I shut the door and quickly placed the knife on the floor by my feet then opened the cupboard under the stairs, listening for any sound of movement from the kitchen, hearing none – not even sobbing, which unnerved me. I quickly found what I needed: an old washing line that I remembered seeing there earlier. I picked it up, tied it securely around the kitchen door knob then trailed it to the banister at the bottom of the stairs where I stretched the line tight and tied the other end around the top of the banister. It was now impossible for her to open the kitchen door. The only other exit was through the back door, which was locked, or the kitchen window, which was securely boarded up. K was trapped. She wasn't going anywhere and I had the keys.

Relief sang through my veins like water through a parched vine, but I didn't slow down. I ran upstairs into my bedroom where Emma lay curled up, her eyes wide and terrified, her nightgown in her mouth.

"Get up," I said, "we're leaving now."

Emma got out of bed, sensing my no-nonsense tone, and watched me grab my pillow and bed covers, which I dragged down the stairs. I placed the pillow under Patrick's head and covered him with my blankets. He was unconscious but still breathing. There was no way on earth Emma and I could carry him anywhere fast enough, so we would have to leave him there while we went to get help.

"Is the man okay?" Emma whispered.

I nodded and dashed to the front door, hesitating. We had no supplies – I hadn't been able to find the holdall I needed to stash my collection of tins in. How far was it to the nearest house? I didn't know.

I grabbed Emma's hand and pulled her after me back upstairs.

"Go to the toilet then drink as much water as you can," I said. She followed my instructions and I went into her room to find her slippers or, if possible, any outdoor shoes Mother may have bought her.

In the spare room, I saw how Mother had escaped. She had hacked through the sown up middle of the curtains – with what I couldn't be sure – then smashed the glass - s*o she hadn't nailed boards over Clarabelle's window* - and jumped out. The drop was big; she had been extremely lucky not to break any bones.

In the wardrobe, I found a pair of black plimsolls which I slid onto Emma's feet. I pulled a blue doll dress on over her nightgown, hoping the two garments together would be enough to keep her warm.

Emma stayed as quiet as a mouse, watching me with her huge, bleary eyes while I emptied my bladder then drank as much water from the tap as I could. We had to stay hydrated. If necessary, we could go without food for a while, but water was essential. I looked down at my slippers – they would have to do. At least they had hard soles. Mother's feet were bigger than mine, so wearing her shoes would only slow us down, and we had to move as fast as possible for Patrick's sake.

We ran downstairs and I tried a couple of keys before finding the right one. With a deep, shaky breath, I slotted the key into the keyhole and unlocked the front door.

Chapter Twenty

Outside. I was standing outside. I was outside for the first time in ten years. I thought my cheeks would break I was smiling so hard. Greens and browns and blues and light – so much light. Natural light that was warm yet fresh, so fresh it made the fine hairs on my body tingle. I shivered with pleasure, wincing against the sun though it remained hidden behind a white frosting of cloud.

I wanted this moment to last, wanted to feel, taste, smell, hear every atom of it. I inhaled the air, filling my lungs with the stuff, savouring, relishing, loving everything. Even the red car was a wonderful sight to behold with its gleaming scarlet brightness, its bonnet shimmering with light. The ground was hard earth; natural, not man-made. And the trees that loomed larger than the cottage which I did not want to turn and see - the trees were magnificent. So tall and green and full of colour and life. I could hear birds chattering to each other, see ants on the ground, clouds in the sky. My head ached with the brightness but I was not in any real pain. My skin was not melting off or beginning to burn or peel or do any of the many other horrible things I had imagined. My eyes were not bursting, my body was not on fire, my lungs had not exploded in my chest. I was alive and breathing and healthy. I grinned down at Emma and she gave me a small smile.

"Can I go home now?" she said.

"We have a little way to go, but yes, we're going home."

Hand in hand we strode past the car, taking the dirt road, following the tyre tracks that Mother's car had so recently created. We walked quickly along the dusty road, me shielding my eyes with my free hand and scanning the distance, unsurprised to see nothing more than dirt road, trees on either side of us and far, far in the distance, a bright green field. I had seen some of this from Mother's bedroom window.

After about twenty minutes, a sheen had worked its way onto my skin, Emma's too.

"I'm tired. How long 'til we get there?"

I shrugged. "I don't know, but we can't stop. Patrick's not very well. We need to find someone who can help him as quickly as possible."

"What's wrong with him?"

I hesitated, unsure how much to tell her, whether to lie or tell the truth. I'd had enough of lies to last a lifetime - but Emma was only five years old. She had been through so much already. Too much.

Unbidden, the sight of Patrick grasping his side, appealing to Mother, blood soaking through his T-shirt into the carpet, flashed into my mind's eye. I shivered despite the warmth, unable to believe all that had happened. Unable to believe I had managed to escape.

I dropped my arm to my side and looked at the bunch of keys in my palm. I was holding them so tightly that they were cutting into my palm. I loosened my grip and glanced at Emma's damp hair.

"Patrick got hurt," I said.

"How?"

"Mother hit him and he fell over."

Emma looked up at me. "Oh. Is she a bad lady?"

"Yes, but she can't hurt us anymore. We're free. Everything will be okay now. Shall we go a little faster? Remember, Patrick needs us to find someone to help him."

Emma nodded.

We picked up our pace, breaking into a half-run. The clouds drifted off the sun, which beat down on us making sweat drip down our faces and backs, but we kept up the pace, Emma's sweaty hand in my sweaty hand, which burned and throbbed from the bleach and my unhealed wound.

The dirt road seemed to go on forever as did the woods on either side. I considered branching off the road into the woods to look for a footpath of some kind that might lead us to a house or farm. The woods looked dense though and the fear of getting lost prevented me from following that idea. Instead, I urged Emma to keep up our half-run and tried to ignore the pains in my thigh muscles. My body was not used to this sort of exercise. Emma seemed to be bearing up better than me.

"Can we sing a song?" she said, smiling up at me.

I was panting now and my instinct was to shake my head but the keenness in her tired eyes made me say yes.

"Which one?" I said, knowing that I did not know many songs.

"Twinkle Twinkle Little Star," she said and she began to sing.

Mother had sung this song to me before bed when I was little. The thought was disturbing. Memories of Mother reading me bedtime stories drifted into my head and I crushed them, fighting the strange, sick feeling that accompanied the memories. Sometimes she had been so loving, such a good mother. It had been easy to believe her lies when I was younger, when I was her perfect little doll.

I joined in with Emma's song and we ran hand in hand along the dirt road, Mother's keys jangling in my free hand, my head aching from the light and my toes blistering from my loose slippers. I dropped the keys. I wouldn't need them anymore.

After a while, we slowed to a walk to catch our breath and Emma sang a song that I had never heard of before which she said was from 'Chitty Chitty Bang Bang' - a book of children's songs or nursery rhymes I assumed. She let go of my hand and skipped away singing, her tiredness suddenly gone as if the song had given her a burst of energy and happiness. She clearly didn't know all of the words, so she kept singing the same couple of lines over and over again. I found myself smiling as she skipped ahead, wondering if I would ever feel that kind of happiness again. Would I find my real parents? Were they even still alive? If they weren't, what would happen to me?

"Emma – can you hear that?" I said, stopping and straining my ears. Emma carried on singing.

"Emma! Stop!" I said sharply.

She turned around, wide-eyed, chest heaving.

I could hear something in the distance. Something coming from behind us.

"Can you hear that?" I said.

Emma nodded. "Yes. It's a car."

"A car?" I turned around back the way we had come, heart slamming against my ribs.

Speeding toward us was a red car. Mother's car.

Chapter Twenty-One

My first thought was *how did she get out?* My second thought was *run.* I grabbed Emma's wrist and dragged her to the left, towards the woods, thinking quickly: the car would not be able to go into the densely packed trees, which meant Mother would have to leave the car and follow on foot.

I glanced over my shoulder to see the car stop, skidding slightly, pale brown dust puffing into the air. Emma and I ran down a steep, grassy bank into the trees. The slam of the car door told me Mother was not going to give up. In my mind, I pictured her sprinting after us, her face twisted with rage, blood covering her clothes, a knife glinting in her hand. I could not be certain she held a weapon but my gut told me she would not have come unprepared. If she caught up with us, a knife would be the perfect way of persuading us to come along quietly.

At my side, Emma slipped and stumbled over a thick root. She gasped and cried, slowing down, forcing me to pause to pick her up. Her face was pale and sweaty, her eyes wide with terror.

"Hold on tightly with your arms and legs," I panted. I was already short of breath and though Emma weighed very little, I was not strong. She clung to me so tightly though that she felt like a second skin. Her small body trembled and vibrated with tension against mine and I could feel her heartbeat thrumming against my chest. I wanted to reassure her that everything was going to be okay. I opened my mouth to speak as a scream tore through the air behind us.

"MIRABELLE! STOP!"

Emma jumped in my arms and clung on even tighter, making herself lighter but compressing my lungs. Panting for breath, I darted between the towering trees and leapt over a fallen tree trunk and ran on, using my right arm for balance, wrapping the other around Emma. Obstacles appeared out of nowhere. The woods were as horribly unpredictable as Mother. Thorn bushes and spiky leaves scratched and tore at my bare arms and legs and dress. My slippers were long gone, lost when we rushed down the bank. I knew my feet were cut and bleeding. I dreaded to think of the wealth of grime being crushed and pressed into my bloodied feet, but my adrenaline surge seemed to have made any kind of pain vanish. That was one blessing at least.

Clouds covered the sun, submerging the woods in shadows and giving my eyes the chance to stop watering. Everything turned a few shades darker and a few degrees cooler. My breaths came in ragged gasps. I knew I could not keep up this pace for much longer. Emma's arms and legs loosened and she grew heavier, her body dipping toward the ground, her hands pulling on my neck, her body bouncing up and down with every stride I took.

"Hold on – tighter," I gasped.

She responded but not as well as before. She was weakening and so was I. But I could not stop. I could not let her catch up with us. I thought about Patrick and pushed harder. My legs were heavy. I wrapped both arms around Emma and held her against me. My arms protested from the weight as she sank into them. I was going to have to put her down soon and hope that she could run fast enough.

A low branch came out of nowhere and I ducked just in time, then tripped and fell, throwing out my hands to stop myself from hitting the ground face first. Emma cried out but clung on as we fell. Her back hit the ground though not hard. My arms jarred with the force of the fall. I gritted my teeth and told Emma she'd have to run now. She let go of me and pushed herself to her feet, slotting her hand into mine. We ran. In the distance I could see light penetrating the trees. The woods were coming to an end. Beyond the trees lay a field. A field would be easier to run through – for us and for Mother. But maybe someone would be in the field. A farmer perhaps.

My lungs burned. Emma was too slow. I considered carrying her again but that would mean stopping to pick her up. Was Mother still following us? There had been no more yells. No more terrifying screams.

Unable to resist, I glanced back. Mother was nowhere to be seen. I frowned and faced forward. Had she given up? Had she fallen over? Twisted her ankle?

The thought was like the feeling of hot water on aching muscles but I fought the urge to slow down and carried on running, pulling Emma along behind me. And there was the light – more light – shining through the gaps between the trees. And green – so much green. I could see the field. Not long now until we broke out of the woods into open air. Out of this hell hole of nature's obstacles.

But at the edge of the woods we reached a fence topped with silver barbs of wire which ran as high as my waist. I stopped, picked up Emma and heaved her over the fence, lifting her as high as I could to avoid the barbs.

"Keep running," I said. She shook her head. I shouted at her to move and she jumped. Tears sprang to her eyes and her chin wobbled.

"I don't want to leave you," she said.

I nodded, not wanting to waste time arguing, and carefully placed my hand on a small section of wire between the barbed knots, noticing further up the fence a clump of white wool snagged on a barb. My heart leapt; wool meant sheep; sheep meant farmers; farmers meant help.

I swung my leg over the fence, pushing down on the wire with my hand. The fence wobbled and I fell, tearing my other leg on a barb as it followed my body onto the grass. A sharp pain speared my calf. I looked down, wincing. The vicious metal had ripped a three inch cut down my leg. Blood dribbled out and down my leg like water out of a tap.

"Are you okay?" Emma said.

I nodded, taking her hand. The pain was bad, but not bad enough to stop me. I glanced backward, saw nothing but trees. Emma looked around too.

"She's gone," Emma said quietly.

I could hear the hope in her voice, almost like she couldn't believe our luck. For me too, the idea that Mother had gone was too good to be true, and I knew that we had to keep on running until we found someone. If we stopped for too long and she was still around, she might catch up and grab us. I couldn't – *wouldn't* – go back to that place. And Patrick needed help.

"We need to keep running," I said to Emma, "Okay?"

She nodded bravely and we ran through the ankle-high grass toward the once more burning sun.

Chapter Twenty-Two

We ran through the green field into another field and another. The third field had recently been ploughed; immense tractor tracks and some kind of huge machinery had churned up the earth turning the field into one gigantic ocean of dry, hard, undulating soil.

Did this mean we were close to making human contact? My heart leapt and I thought I might die with hope – and fear. What if the person we met was damaged too? How many people in the world were damaged like Mother? If she was damaged, there had to be others. I felt my hope sink as a realisation set in: ultimately, we had no choice. We would have to place our trust in the first person - or people - we saw. I knew this and it frightened me badly. But Patrick had been good. Sceptical, but kind. He had tried to help us, even though he had struggled to believe my story. Would others think I was making it up too? Would they take us back there? Back to that secret house in the middle of nowhere? I shuddered. Just thinking about it made me want to scream.

Emma stumbled on the uneven earth and I held up her wrist,

preventing her from falling.

"Thank you," she said, looking up at me through misty eyes.

"We're going to be fine. I promise," I said, trying to make my voice calm.

I had to stop thinking the worst.

It seemed like Mother had given up. We had escaped the cottage. We were outside. Free. I wasn't dying anymore – not that I ever had been. I was alive and well and going to find my parents and live happily ever after, like they did in fairytales. Emma was going to go back to her parents and forget all about the last four weeks of her life. One day she would look back on it all and it would feel like one really bad nightmare. She was so young that she would forget all about this horrible experience. She wasn't physically hurt. Mother had never harmed her, except for that bruise on her arm the day she took her from the supermarket.

My heart calmed a little. I pushed damp strands of hair out of my eyes, pasting them to the sweaty hair on top of my head, and shielded my gaze from the sun. Up ahead, at the top end of the next field stood a few buildings. I blinked several times, desperate to believe what I was seeing, to clear the stinging tears from my eyes. Was it a mirage or was it real?

Emma jumped up and down pointing, "Look, Polly! Look!"

"I know," I said, beaming down at her. It was real. A real, bricks and mortar farm. Just like the ones I'd seen in books.

Emma grinned at me and squealed. We ran over the mud dunes using the last dregs of our energy, the sun doing its best to slow us down and losing as we flew across the dirt, carried by hope and excitement, propelled by expectancy. Anticipation blasted away some of my concerns and I felt my face relax - we were going to find someone who could help us, help Patrick. Someone grown up and sensible and responsible and full of knowledge about what to do in a situation like this. They would call the police and the police would go to the cottage and they would find Patrick and he would still be alive and they would rush him to a hospital and the doctors at the hospital would save him, and then, when I had been reunited with my parents and Emma with hers, Emma and I would go and visit Patrick in the hospital and take him a present to thank him for helping us get away. And Mother would be in a special place where they take care of damaged people and I'd never have to see her ever again...

We slowed to a walk when we got within yards of the farm. There were three buildings in total. The first building was a small house with a low, tile-topped roof and pebbly walls that were an unhealthy off-white colour. We approached from the back of the house and entered an open patch of barren land upon which stood two other buildings and a large metal cage. There were two large, black dogs in the cage which immediately stood up and pressed their faces against the metal wire, baring their teeth and snarling. A third dog lay on the ground chomping on a huge bone. The dog was attached to the biggest outbuilding by a long, thick, metal chain. It was sturdy and muscular with a sloping face and white fur. It paid us no attention other than a couple of glances, too interested in its bone to bother with us.

Emma hugged my side and shook her head. "I don't like it here."

I stared where she was staring. The building opposite had a corrugated roof and it was locked, a heavy-looking chain and padlock keeping the doors tightly shut, but the door of the building that the dog was chained to stood ajar a few inches. In and out of the opening buzzed hundreds and hundreds of flies.

"What's in *there*?" Emma whispered.

"I don't know," I murmured, turning to the small house.

The door was painted dark green and the paint was peeling. A brass door knocker in the shape of a horse's head stared at me. I hesitated then raised my hand and banged the horse head three times. We waited, Emma's hand trembling ever-so-slightly in mine. Clouds blocked the sun pooling us in shadow. I knocked again. Louder, more urgently, straining my ears for the sound of footsteps behind the door.

"Let's go," Emma whined.

"No," I said, knocking a third time.

"Hello!" I called.

I tried the door, barely touching the door knob, and the door swung inward with a long, high-pitched creak. I took a tentative step forward and peered into the gloomy interior of the house.

"Hello?" I tried again.

"Maybe we can find a telephone," Emma said, her voice smaller than ever.

I looked at her. "Yes – where will it be?"

"What?"

"The telephone?"

"We keep ours in the lounge at home."

"Okay, great. So if we can find a phone, we can talk to someone who might help us. We can call the police."

Emma nodded. "Yes. The numbers are nine, nine, nine. Mummy and Daddy teached me them."

"That's brilliant," I said smiling at her, "Come on."

I pulled her into the house, leaving the door open behind us. We were in a small kitchen. The counters were a mess; covered with dirty plates and dirty saucepans and mugs, filling the room with an unpleasant smell a bit like sour milk. I flicked on a light but it didn't come on.

"The telephone won't be in here," Emma said.

We left the kitchen and crossed a small hallway. I opened one of two doors that led off from the hallway and we entered a room with a small bed in it. The bed was unmade and a few pairs of men's underwear dotted the floor. The room smelt like bad breath and body odour. There was no window in the room. I grimaced, backed out and shut the door. We tried the next and final door in the small house and I smiled, pleased to see a living room of sorts. A black box with a window in it sat on top of a table at the back of the room. A television maybe. Like telephones, I had read about televisions but never seen one. Facing the black box was a brown, one-seater sofa. Beer cans littered the floor around the sofa and magazines lay on a table in the centre of the room. On the table beneath the window sat a black, square object with numbered buttons on. It had to be the telephone.

Emma let go of my hand and ran over to the odd contraption. She picked part of it up and waved it at me.

"Telephone!" she said.

I walked over and took hold of the plastic black thing she was holding.

"Hold it to your ear and I'll do the numbers," Emma said excitedly.

I did as she asked, feeling strange, uncomfortable, not sure I was doing it right. Emma nodded at me as I placed one of the round end parts to my ear and the other round part to my mouth. She stabbed the number nine on the machine three times and I heard something beep. Then I heard a ringing sound. Then a voice, but the voice wasn't coming from the telephone; it was coming from behind me.

Chapter Twenty-Three

"Who the hell are you?"

I jumped and dropped the telephone. It fell to the carpet with a thud, a black, curling wire snaking up from the ground to the machine on the table. Vaguely I registered a crackly voice coming from the ground, but the voice in the room seemed to reverberate inside my skull.

I span around, inhaling sharply.

A man with a large, round stomach stood just inside the living room doorway. He was dirty-looking, his white vest stained and too tight across his belly. He wore badly fitting blue jeans and no shoes, only dirty socks with holes in the toes. Long, dark hairs poked out of the top of his vest. Even in the gloomy room I could make out dark circles under his eyes and red blotches on his bulbous nose. His hair was long, dark and stringy and he had a thick, bushy beard. Down by his side he clutched a bulging carrier bag.

"We – er – we-" I tried to speak, but the man held up one large hand.

"Give it me!" he barked, lurching into the room.

"Give you *what*?" I said.

"Whatever you've stole," he said.

"We haven't stolen anything," I said, pushing Emma behind me, "Please, we just want-"

"Come here!" he shouted.

I froze and clamped my mouth shut. He swayed visibly and I realised he was drunk. He let the bag drop to the floor then cursed and bent over, scrabbling to pick up beer cans as they rolled across the carpet.

"Please, sir," I said, "Please may we use your phone? That's all. We weren't stealing. I promise."

He didn't seem to hear me. Still swearing, he lurched upright clutching a can of beer and teetered out of the room. I looked down at the telephone piece that lay on the carpet, its twisty chain spiralling upward like some kind of bizarre umbilical cord. I could hear a faint dead-sounding tone coming from it and wondered what that meant. Before I could do or say anything, Emma crouched down and grabbed the telephone bit then replaced it on its machine on the table.

"We can try again," she whispered, tugging me round.

"No," I said, "We need to get out of here."

I pulled her out of the room into the hallway. We crept up the small, narrow corridor toward the kitchen. This man was drunk so there was no telling what he might do. I knew a little about alcohol and it was enough to make me wary. Mother had told me everything I knew about it, but I felt quite sure having now seen this man and the way he was behaving, that what she had told me about alcohol was the truth. Not everything she had told me was a lie. Most of it, but not all. A strange pain squeezed my heart. I shook my head, told myself to concentrate. We had to get out of this place, find someone who was capable of helping us. This man was acting strangely. He was drunk. He was not trustworthy. Not in the slightest bit.

He had his back to us when we reached the kitchen. I could see the crack in his bottom. It was gross. He stood in front of the oven humming to himself. A tune I had never heard. I didn't think it sounded like ABBA anyway. It was too slow for that.

I tried to think straight. We had to get away. If we were quiet and quick, we could creep past without him seeing us and get out.

I hesitated a second, another second, and another, then yanked Emma into the room and toward the door that led outside. Emma tripped, making a scuffling sound. He whirled around, a wooden spoon raised in his meaty fist, a cry bursting from his lips. He reached out and grabbed my shoulder as I pushed Emma forward.

"Go!" I yelled - but she didn't. She stopped and turned around, tears welling in her eyes.

"Come here!" the man bellowed, grabbing Emma's arm. He pulled her towards himself and pushed us out of the kitchen back into the hallway.

"You're not going anywhere yet, girlies," he said with a chuckle that turned into a gurgling cough.

He pushed our backs, forcing us into the living room, shouting at us to sit on the sofa. We did as he commanded. He whirled around and headed back toward the kitchen. I pulled Emma onto my lap and hugged her close, whispering reassuring things in her ear, trying to keep the tremors out of my voice. The fear and worry.

What was he going to do to us? Why wouldn't he let us go? Mother's talk of men with vile sexual appetites crawled into my mind, and for a split second I found myself wishing the most unimaginable thing: that I'd never found out that she wasn't my real mother. If I hadn't found out we wouldn't be here right now; we would be back in the cottage, our food, beds and clothes provided for us, our basic needs met...

But ignorance *wasn't* bliss and she was ill in the head. I knew that. I did. But right now, I would rather be in Mother's company than this man's. If he wanted to, he could do worse to us than Mother. Much worse...

My body began to shake. I couldn't help it. Couldn't stop the tremors from taking over my limbs. Emma was trembling too. I pulled her closer and she buried her head in my shoulder and began to cry.

Think. Think.

A greasy meat smell wafted into the room.

I looked at the window above the small table. The window was small, but I wasn't exactly huge. Emma would definitely fit through. I glanced back at the door to the living room. He wasn't back yet, but we didn't have much time until he joined us. I didn't know how I knew, but I knew.

"Get up!" I whispered sharply, pushing Emma up.

I ran to the window and unlatched it. It opened about a hand's width. Emma would fit through, but would I?

I hoisted her up and helped her slide herself through the narrow space between the window frame and the window itself. She fell to the ground on her hands and knees and looked back at me, panic making her eyes wider than ever.

"Polly?"

"Go," I said.

She stared dumbly at me, still on her hands and knees. I pulled myself onto the sill and tried to slide through, but my chest was too wide. I couldn't go with her.

"Go!" I screamed.

She shook her head and grabbed at my hands.

I pushed her away, looking into her eyes, "Run, Emma. Get help. Find someone. Tell them where I am. And about Patrick. Go!"

Tears spilled down her cheeks. She hiccupped, her face scrunching up into an unrecognisable version of itself, then she turned and fled.

Chapter Twenty-Four

I immediately regretted what I'd done. If Emma couldn't find anyone she would die of dehydration or starvation. She wouldn't know how to find water or food in the wilderness and it was hot out there. Too hot. What if the heat became too much and she fainted and a wild dog came along and...I bit my lip so hard it hurt, unable to complete the thought, fighting the horrific scene that pushed its way into my mind. Other images collided with each other: Mother finding Emma, dragging her back to the cottage, punishing her for running away, or, worse still, someone as awful as the man in this house finding her, taking her back to his house, torturing her, murdering her...

For a second I thought I was going to be sick. I bent over and focused on breathing. Working myself into a state was pointless. I had to think.

"Hey! Where's the other one gone?"

I span around. In one hand the man held a plate piled high with slabs of fatty meat and steaming potatoes. In the other hand he held a can of beer. He took a long swig from the can then entered the room, kicking the door closed behind him and nearly losing his balance.

"Hey! I asked you a question!" he barked. He made his way to the sofa, kicking empty cans out of his path.

"She's gone. Out there," I said softly.

He eased himself down, groaning as he did so and took another swig of beer then placed the can between his right knee and the arm of the sofa and began to shovel meat and potatoes into his mouth, barely chewing before swallowing down the food noisily. He followed every couple of mouthfuls with a swig of alcohol.

"Gone has she? Shame. Least I've still got you," he chuckled throatily then burped.

"Please, sir," I tried, "please can I use your telephone?"

"Who're you so desperate to call?" he said, not looking up from his plate.

I paused. Should I lie or tell the truth?

I swallowed, wiped sweat off my forehead with the back of my trembling hand. "My parents. Emma and I got lost in the woods..."

He nodded and looked at me. His eyes looked strange, almost like jiggling marbles. A memory of Mother and I playing with marbles entered my head followed by one of us playing with conkers tied to string. Sometimes she had been fine. My heart hurt and then I thought about how she had treated me those last couple of days – how she had lied to me for so long – made me believe I was dying. Anger tore through me and I stared straight at the man.

"Let me use the telephone or let me leave," I said as confidently as I could, crossing my arms and lifting my chin, trying to stand tall.

He shovelled the last mouthful of his meal into his mouth and drained the beer can. He burped again and wiped his mouth with the back of his hand.

"Alright, alright. You're not using my phone, but you can go - after I check something."

He put his plate on the floor beside the chair and stood up, swaying slightly. The beer can fell to the ground, the last couple of drops oozing onto the carpet.

"Come here," he said, slurring his words. He curled his finger at me and beckoned me toward him.

"Wh-wh-why?"

"'Cos I've got to check you 'ain't stole nothin'. Come here."

"I haven't stolen anything. I already told you that."

"COME HERE!" he bellowed the words so loudly that the ground seemed to quake. I jumped and obeyed, walking slowly, fighting tears.

"What's this stupid thing you're wearin'?" he said, waving his hand at my brown sack dress.

I didn't reply. I stopped a little way from him.

He chuckled and rubbed his groin. I wanted to run but knew if I moved now, he would reach out and grab me. Instead, I stared defiantly up at his jiggling eyes as they raked over my dress.

"Can't see anything hid away from here," he said. He smiled and licked his lips.

"Come closer. I've got to do a body check. I used to be a bouncer, ya know!" he wheezed out a laugh, clutching his huge gut as if he'd told the best joke in the world. When he had recovered, he beckoned me closer again.

I didn't move. He stepped forward, bringing us so close that his foul body odour enveloped my whole body. From here, I could see an intricate network of spiky red veins on his nose and cheeks.

Black hairs sprouted out of his bulbous nose above dry, cracked lips.

"Lift up your arms like this," he said, raising his arms to the sides, "and stand like this." He stepped out one foot in a clumsy movement, making his stance very wide.

I hesitated. A mad thought seized me and I kicked him as hard as I could in his groin. He roared with pain and doubled over. I ran for the door, yanked it open, darted up the hallway into the kitchen, opened the other door and sprinted out of the house.

The black dogs snapped their jaws and barked viciously as I ran past, but they were caged and I was free. I didn't spare them a second look as I ran past the man's rusty blue truck and headed in the direction that Emma had gone.

Chapter Twenty-Five

The sun blinded me, my leg throbbed and my feet left bloody prints on the pale, cracked earth. Every few seconds, I glanced over my shoulder convinced I was being followed by the drunken man from the farm. I had made it to the next patch of land, which was more a desert than a field. The ground was hard and rough with the occasional clump of sprouting vegetation, so dry and hot beneath my sore feet that it felt like I was running on baked sandpaper. My soles were burning and the pain was becoming unbearable. Not too far away though, beyond this barren stretch, I could see a bright yellow field. Surely, the ground there would be cooler, moister.

I glanced back. Heard no-one. Saw no-one. But I couldn't stop shaking.

"Emma!" I shouted her name over and over again until my voice cracked.

There was no sign anywhere of Emma and I realised with rising dread that anything could have happened to her. She could have fallen into a ditch and been knocked unconscious or fallen and broken her ankle. She might have been shot by a farmer, angry that someone was on his private land. Anything could have happened to her. Anything. And it was my fault. I never should have pushed her out of that window.

I slowed down and put my hands on my knees, sucking in huge, warm, pollen-scented lungfuls of air. Midges buzzed around my head and I waved them away and took another moment, one hand shielding my eyes, the other shooing off the persistent flies. I scanned the horizon. Saw nothing but fields – and then, far away, five fields away in a north-east direction from here, a patch of red caught my eye. Was it another farm? A house? It was definitely a building of some kind.

I should have started running towards it, but I didn't. I froze. Span around, suddenly certain I could hear a car coming. I listened and listened, but all I heard was the whiny cry of the flies pestering me. There was no-one chasing me. Not anymore. The drunken man was probably still lying on the ground writhing around in agony. A naughty sensation of satisfaction rippled through me as I remembered the shock and pain in his eyes. I didn't feel guilty. He had deserved it, and if he came for me, I would do it again and again.

My breath was back so, wincing, I ran on, climbing over a wooden gate into the yellow field, which smelt so strong it made my head fuzzy and my nose run. The yellow plants were as tall as my waist but not so tough that I couldn't run through them. The ground was softer and cooler here offering my injured feet a little respite. I ran through the field and climbed over another wooden gate into the next field which hosted five brown cows and one calf that could not have been very old at all. The cows stared at me as one and I took a wide berth, instinctively steering clear of them in case they thought I presented a threat to the little calf. The calf tried to gambol over to me but one of the adult cows blocked its path.

I dodged a pile of dung and climbed over another wooden gate. I was now only three fields away. Countryside stretched out on all sides of me and I found myself relaxing enough to admire how beautiful and glowing the landscape was; colours so vivid they hurt; colours so vivid they brought joy into my heart. This field was another grass field and easier on my feet. I ran faster, flying over the grass, pumping my arms and legs until I reached the end of the field which was signalled by a barbed wire fence. Taking more time than before, I gingerly climbed over the fence, pausing for breath on the other side then walking forward. This was another grass field, abandoned I thought, until I saw it: a bull. The bull was black and huge. It had its back to me, so I thought I'd chance it. I ran straight up the middle of the field, cursing my feet as the pain mounted. I was almost there when I heard hooves slamming the ground. Glancing back, I saw with horror that the bull was heading for me, head down, horns forward. I threw myself through the middle section of a different kind of fence, crying out as it electrocuted me, sending needles of pain stabbing all over my hands and arms from where I'd made contact. The bull slowed to a halt inches from the fence and glared at me, snorting, its nostrils flaring, hooves scuffing the ground.

I scrambled to my feet and limped through the last field, relieved to find the stabbing pains gone after a few seconds and happy to note that this field held nothing but sheep and lambs, who all skittered away when I approached.

And there it was: a red brick building. A very big house by the look of it. An expensive, well-looked-after house. A house that was completely different to the one I'd come from. Did that mean the owner would be completely different? Despite everything, hope flared inside me. I was so tired, so in need of rest. My feet were in shreds and I could barely walk another step. I felt tears sting my eyes; this could be the end of it all. The pain and fear and danger could finally be over.

But I had to remain cautious. A shiny black car sat parked on a white pebble drive facing the front of the house. On the other side of the car was a big patch of grass with a white horse standing in the centre. The horse was watching me. I looked up the drive and saw that it led to a road. A real road, not a dirt road. My heart sang; I had reached civilisation. At long last, I was near a town – a place where I could find the police.

Crouching low, I pushed open a large swing gate and darted through. I dashed over to the car and hid behind it, peering round at the house, trying to work out whether it was safe.

The house had a large white door and red brick walls. A pretty white and black sign reading: Greenfield House had been nailed to the wall beside the front door. Two hanging pots of flowers hung from either side of the door making the place seem warm and inviting. It looked so civilised. So posh. So *light*. The curtains were drawn open in all four windows: the two downstairs and the two upstairs. There were no boards, no tape, no efforts made to conceal anything. This was a regular, nice, happy home, I felt sure of it.

Exhaling to steady my nerves, I left my hiding place and limped to the front door. I raised my hand to knock but someone opened the door, making me jump.

Chapter Twenty-Six

"Oh my!"

An elderly woman with short white hair that curled neatly under her chin answered the door. She was small and thin, wearing a floaty, mint-green dress. A white shawl was draped across her narrow shoulders. I could smell something overly sweet and thought it must be her perfume. Her wrinkled hands flew to her mouth as she took in my appearance. I stared back at her, wondering what she saw when she looked at me. What she was thinking. She gripped the door frame and for a moment I thought she was going to slam the door in my face.

"Harold! Harold!" she shouted, turning round, her voice hoarse.

She turned back to me and said gently, "Wait here a moment, dear. I must get Harold."

"Who's Harold?" I said, but she had already retreated into the house leaving the door wide open.

Beyond the door was a dark wood floor and a few steps away was a staircase with a white banister. There was nothing on the floor. No beer cans in sight. Only a clean, floral smell.

A grey cat with pale green eyes appeared in the doorway. It stared at me for a few seconds then clearly decided I didn't pose a threat. I watched in wonder as it curled itself around my ankles, purring, its body vibrating as I leant over to stroke its silky-soft fur. I suddenly felt light-headed, the urge to lie down overwhelming. I leant against the wall beside the front door and closed my eyes.

A sound made me look up. A tall, grey-haired man with a long face and angular body eyed me up and down. He wore blue jeans and a short-sleeved white shirt which looked clean. He smelt clean too and his eyes didn't jiggle; they looked directly at me. These eyes were a sober, bright blue and right now they were wide with what I thought was concern.

"Come in, child, come in," he said, stepping back and beckoning me into the house, his voice low and serious. "Dot, go and make her a glass of milk and something to eat."

"What's your name?" he said, closing the door behind me.

I had to think for a moment. I hesitated. Should I tell him my real name? What if he knew Mother? What if they were friends? But then I pictured Mother in this room talking with this elderly couple and the picture didn't make sense.

He seemed to sense my reluctance and shook his head, "It's fine. You don't have to tell me. Come on into the living room. Let's give those feet a rest."

Numbly, I followed him into a large room with a yellow and orange-patterned carpet and matching curtains. The walls were white and they looked clean too. Clean and light. I wanted to tell the man – Harold – that I liked his house. I opened my mouth to speak as the old lady – Dot - rushed into the room holding a tray. I sat down on a squishy cream sofa, immediately relishing the lack of pressure on my feet.

"Drink some milk, dear," Dot said, passing me a glass.

I did as she told me, spilling milk down my chin and onto myself and not caring. The cold, fresh milk felt wonderful against my dry throat and I smiled at her gratefully.

"Thank you," I said.

"Oh dear. Look at your poor feet. I'll fetch something to clean those, shall I Harold?"

Harold nodded, his eyes never leaving me.

"You need to call the police," I said, taking a small bite of the sandwich that Dot had made me.

"Okay," he said, scratching his chin, "can you tell me why?"

I took another bite of sandwich, chewed it quickly. It was amazing what a little milk and bread could do for energy levels. I felt more awake and sat up straighter.

"There's a man. Patrick. He's hurt. He needs help. And there's Emma. I don't know where she is and it's my fault – I never should have told her to go. I-"

"Take a breath," Harold said, "Tell me who Patrick is first."

"He's this man who showed up at the cottage and then I got him involved and she stabbed him and-"

"Who stabbed him?"

"Mother. I don't know her real name. She's not well. She needs help too but not as much as Patrick. He's dying."

"Okay, okay. What about Emma? Tell me about her."

"She's only five. She's out there alone, all alone and she's so little, so scared - and it's all my fault!"

I started to cry, tried to stop, knowing I needed to explain better, but completely unable to fight the sobs that took over my eyes and mind and body. I tasted salt. I vaguely registered a hand on my shoulder and someone taking the plate out of my hand and someone with a gentle voice saying soothing things. I vaguely felt myself being made to lie down, being covered with a blanket, someone saying they were going to drive to the police station. I was so tired and the sofa was so comfortable and the blankets so warm and my eyes were heavy, so heavy.

Someone was stroking my forehead.

Murmuring nice things.

Stroking and soothing and stroking and soothing and stroking, stroking, stroking.

Chapter Twenty-Seven

I woke with a start, heart hammering, thinking I was back there, with Mother, trapped in the darkness of the cottage. I sucked in sharp breaths and stared around, my mind slowly piecing things back together. As my eyes adjusted to the gloom and my nose picked up a flowery scent, I remembered where I was: Harold and Dot's house. I wasn't in the cottage anymore. I jerked upright – I hadn't spoken to the police yet – told them about Patrick or Emma! I had let myself fall asleep and now it might be too late to save Patrick or Emma. I dreaded to think what might have happened to little Emma. Out there all alone, just five years old...

I pushed back the bed covers and climbed out of the bed, wincing as my feet took the weight of my body, surprised to see my feet clean and bandaged. Dot. She must have cleaned them while I slept. A surge of gratitude flooded me and I touched the bandages, astonished by her kindness.

The curtains were drawn tightly together. Panic ballooned in my chest; what if they were sown shut? What if boards had been nailed behind those curtains? No. Dot was kind. She was a good person.

I tugged the curtains apart. They opened with ease and I saw a full moon in a starry, navy sky. The sun had set. It was night. How long had I been asleep? How long had Patrick been lying on the floor bleeding out? How long had Emma been wondering around in the wilderness?

I looked down at myself. I was still wearing the brown sack dress but my arms and legs had been wiped clean, the wound on my leg bandaged too. Dot had cleaned every inch of me that she could without taking off my dress. I felt like hugging her.

A glass of water sat on the bedside table. I drained the whole glass then walked to the bedroom door and twisted the knob. The door opened and I slipped out onto a landing which had a green and white flowery carpet. Up here, the lights were off so it was dark. Trailing my hand on the banister, I descended the stairs, pleased to see soft light coming from downstairs. Dot and Harold must still be awake. I remembered suddenly that Harold had driven away to get the police, and realised that Harold and Dot must not have a telephone.

I turned right at the bottom of the stairs and hovered outside the living room. The door was shut. I could hear Dot murmuring to Harold, but no other voices. Alarm crept up my spine. Where were the police?

I hesitated, my hand on the door. Dot and Harold were good, kind people. Maybe the police were on their way. Maybe Harold had told the police then driven back here with the police following him and on the way, the police car had broken down. Yes. That must be why the police weren't here yet. I knew that if the police were here I would hear loud, male, bossy voices. And someone would have woken me up. Someone would be questioning me right this second, desperate to find out everything they could in order to save Patrick and Emma.

Reassured, I pushed open the door and walked into the living room.

Dot was sitting on the sofa, wringing her hands. "Harold ought to be back by now..." She looked up and saw me, stood and rushed across the room.

"You're awake! How are you feeling?" she said gently.

I didn't speak. Couldn't speak. Another woman was in the room sitting on the sofa with her back to me. I couldn't breathe. I knew that body. That long, bony back. That short, blonde hair.

I watched, unable to draw breath.

Mother stood up and turned around, a smile pasted to her thin lips. A smile that did not match the triumphant brightness in her small, dark eyes.

"Mirabelle! Thank the heavens you're alive!" she rushed forward and I staggered backward, putting Dot in between us.

"Mirabelle? Darling, what's wrong? Aren't you happy to see Mummy?"

Dot turned around, her brow crinkling in confusion and concern, "We thought we'd let you sleep a little while longer. Your mother arrived only a few minutes ago. She's been looking all over for you. She's told me all about your father, but don't worry. He's gone now, isn't he Mrs Stone?" Dot looked at Mother then back at me.

"Oh yes. That evil man's gone now. After you ran away, I threatened to call the police and he drove off. You can come home now, little doll. You're safe now."

Mother stepped forward, reaching out a hand to me. I darted around to the other side of Dot and held Dot's hand.

Dot looked down at me, a question in her eyes, the beginnings of doubt entering her mind.

"It's okay now," she said, her eyes flicking from mine to Mother's, "You can go home with your mother now, okay?"

I shook my head. "She's not my mother."

"What? I don't understand," Dot said.

I looked up at the old lady, meeting her eyes, willing her to believe me. "Please make her leave. She's not my mother. She kidnapped me a long time ago. That's why I look like this. That's why I was running away."

Mother laughed and grabbed my free wrist. "What a lot of silly nonsense. Come on, sweetie, you've been through a great ordeal. You-"

"NO!" I shouted, tearing my wrist out of her grip.

Dot pulled me behind herself. She stared at Mother and said in a low voice. "Please, Mrs Stone. The child clearly doesn't want to come with you. The police will be here shortly. Please leave." She opened the living room door, still shielding me with her thin, frail body and gestured with her head toward the front door.

Mother shook her head and stepped towards us. "I'm not leaving without Mirabelle."

"I'm not going with you," I said, trying to hide the fear in my voice.

"Oh yes you are. You are mine. You're coming with me whether you like it or not."

She lunged for me pushing Dot out of the way. Dot stumbled and fell, hitting the ground hard, her hand slipping out of mine. I turned and ran out of the room. Mother grabbed my shoulder and yanked me back, wrapping her arms around my body, holding me to her.

"Stop being so ridiculous, Mirabelle. We're leaving."

I struggled and twisted and turned. She held on tighter, choking the air out of my lungs.

"STOP IT!" she screamed.

I bit her forearm, tasting blood, and she cried out and loosened her grip. I pulled away and stumbled out of the room across the hallway into a large yellow kitchen. I opened the first drawer I could see and pulled out a rolling pin. Turning to face Mother, I raised the block of wood and glared at her.

"Come closer and I'll hurt you," I warned, panting for breath.

Dot appeared in the doorway behind Mother holding a shotgun. The gun looked huge against her tiny, frail form, but Dot's voice was as strong as iron. "Please leave, Mrs Stone. Now."

Mother turned slowly. Everything seemed so unreal all of a sudden. The room fell silent.

"The police will be here soon," Dot said, pointing the gun at Mother, "You need to leave."

"I'm not leaving without my daughter."

"I'm not your daughter," I spat, lowering the rolling pin.

"Yes you are. Mirabelle, you're not well. You are sick. Very sick, and the last few hours' light exposure have made you delirious. I need to get you back home where you'll be safe."

"What's she talking about?" Dot said to me, her eyes leaving Mother.

"She's lying again. She's always lying. She's been lying to me for ten years."

"Oh my God. Ten years?" Dot said, eyes widening.

I nodded. "She took me when I was three years old."

"Shut up!" Mother shouted. She swivelled round to face me. "Where's Emma? What have you done with her?"

I twitched at her use of Emma's real name. It was the first time she'd made that mistake.

"Emma?" Dot said, struggling to catch up, "Is that the little girl you mentioned?"

"Yes. She took Emma too. About a month ago."

Dot gasped. "Emma *Hedges*?"

I nodded eagerly and glanced at Mother, whose face had softened. She suddenly looked a lot older and utterly miserable. Her face seemed to have crumpled in on itself. Her voice turned whiny and pleading and she fell to her knees and clasped her hands in front of her.

"Please, Mirabelle, please Mrs Bancroft. Please, I'm not well. Please don't tell. I just needed her. I love her. I only want to look after her. Make her safe. Make her safer than I was when I was a little girl."

She dissolved into sobs and buried her face in her hands. Her bony shoulders crumpled forward and shook violently as she sobbed.

"But she's not your daughter and neither am I," I said, feeling, despite everything, a small pang of pity, "You can't take other people's children."

Dot lowered the gun and stepped forward. She mouthed the words 'you okay?' to me. I nodded. My whole body sagged and I leaned against the counter.

"Harold will be back soon," Dot murmured.

We watched Mother sob. She rolled onto her side on the kitchen floor still hiding her face in her hands. I felt a strange desire to comfort her and resisted it. I looked at the clock on the wall. It was midnight. Where were the police? Where was Harold? Why wasn't he back yet?

As if reading my thoughts, Dot muttered, "Where is he? What's taking him so long?"

She turned to glance back at the front door and Mother launched herself at the gun, ripping it out of Dot's grasp and pulling Dot onto her hands and knees. She smashed Dot around the face with the barrel of the gun. I heard a crunch as Dot's jaw broke and she toppled onto her side, unconscious.

With a scream I threw myself at Mother, raising the rolling pin over my head in both hands. But she was too quick. She hit my side with the gun, winding me. I staggered to the side and she tore the rolling pin out of my hands and tossed it to the ground. She wrapped her arm around my neck, still gripping the gun in her free hand and forced me out of the kitchen.

"Open it," she snapped when we reached the front door. She tightened her grip on my neck and I opened the door, gasping for breath.

Mother's car was parked on the drive where the black car had been earlier. She forced me into the passenger seat, pointing the gun at me as she hurried around to the driver's side and got in behind the wheel.

"Strap in," she said.

I did as she said. She stabbed a button and the doors clicked.

"Sit on your hands and don't move. If you move, Mirabelle, I will drive back here, go into that house and kill that old lady."

She put the gun on her lap, strapped herself in and started the engine.

Silent tears rolled down my cheeks as the tyres crunched over the white pebble drive and we reversed away from Greenfield House. Away from hope.

Chapter Twenty-Eight

We drove in silence, and I bit my lip, forced myself to stop crying and huddled over to the door, curling my body as far away from hers as possible.

In the closeness of the car sour sweat radiated off her in one, great, nauseating swell. My hands ached with the desire to grab the gun off her lap, but what would I do with it if I actually managed to grab it? I couldn't shoot her. She had been the closest thing to a mother I had ever known. I could never shoot her. And yet the notion zig-zagged across my thoughts like volts of electricity. Returning to the cottage filled me with blackness, with a kind of dread that was as intense as thoughts of dying. If I did go back to that place, I was as good as dead. I felt sick with panic at the mere thought. Felt blackness cornering my vision; what kind of life was a life behind locked doors where the one person you got to interact with was her? I thought about all of the times I had behaved like her perfect little doll, sat there so quietly and dutifully as she painted my face...I could never go back to being that person. I would rather die.

"You've been very badly behaved recently, Mirabelle," her words sliced the stillness in two, jarring my thoughts, "You're usually such a good doll. I don't know what's gotten into you. I'm just relieved you're alive. The light must not have been strong enough to hurt you."

"I'm *not* allergic to light. I never have been," I said, teeth chattering despite my defiant words. I wanted to be brave, to stand up to her, to fight.

Mother fell silent. My stomach cramped. She accelerated up the road faster and I fought back the urge to throw up.

"Slow down. Please," I said as we swerved round a bend that sent me crashing into the side door.

"I can't. We need to find Clarabelle before something happens to her. Where and when did you last see her?"

Nausea billowed in my throat. "I'm going to be sick. You have to stop."

Mother shook her head. "Hold it in. I'm not stopping. Where did you last see her? Tell me or I'll drive straight back to that house and shoot that woman in the head."

"You wouldn't," I said, "You're not a murderer." As I said the words, I tried to believe them, and a series of images pirouetted around my mind's eye like a death parade; Mother marching up to the house, pulling the door open, looking for Dot, standing over her, smiling and pointing the gun at Dot's stricken face, pulling the trigger, Dot's face exploding, blood and flesh dripping off the walls. Blood and flesh. Dot's decapitated body.

"You saw what happened to Patrick," she said, glancing at me.

I clenched my fists. "How is Patrick? Is he..." I couldn't finish the sentence as another series of gory images attacked.

She shrugged. "I don't know. I didn't stop to check. I've been out here searching for you two all day. You don't know how worried I've been. Now, tell me where you last saw Clarabelle. This is your last chance or I'm turning around and going back to that house."

Up ahead I could see houses and tall lights on the side of the road. Were we in a town? My heartbeat jackhammered. I sat up straighter, staring at every house we passed, pressing my nose to the glass. One of those houses could be my house. My real parents' house. I looked at the car door. It was locked, but maybe...

"You have three seconds to tell me. Three, two-" She slowed the car down.

I turned to her, thoughts of trying the door vanishing, and blurted, "You need to turn around. Go back the way we came. I last saw Emma at a farm a few fields away from Dot and Harold's house. I left her there. I can tell you how to get there, just don't hurt the old lady."

She smiled and glanced at me. "Good doll."

She span the car around, tyres squealing, and sped back up the road.

For a fleeting second I hoped that someone had heard the squealing car and decided to follow us, see what the hurry was all about. But it was night-time and no-one sped after us. Heart sinking, I stared out of the window at the last of the houses as we pulled away from town. I thought about Emma wandering around alone in the middle of the night. I didn't think Mother would hurt Emma. Couldn't believe she was that far gone.

I ran over everything I had told Dot. Had I told her my real name? I had definitely told her about Emma and the fact that I had been kidnapped ten years ago. I gritted my teeth; I had not told Dot anything about the cottage, about where it was. Would the small amount that I had told her be enough information for the police to go on? She had told Dot that her name was Mrs Stone. Could that be useful information? Was that the truth or was that yet another lie?

My stomach began to settle, seemingly grown used to the bumpy journey. I looked at the gun on her lap. I could easily reach it.

"Where now?" her voice cut through my thoughts.

We were edging past Greenfield House. The large, white door was still open, the lights still on. No black car sat in the drive. Harold wasn't back yet.

"It's five fields in that direction," I said, pointing.

Her eyes lit up. She smiled at me. "I know it! The knacker's yard. Good doll."

Emma wasn't there but Mother didn't know that. Somehow, if I could work it, maybe I could get away when she went into the drunken man's house to look for Emma. Maybe I could get away, find Emma on my own and get to the police before Patrick died. Maybe not all hope was lost. Maybe.

Swallowing thickly, I tried to work out what to do, discarding idea after idea. The main problem was the gun. I didn't think she'd shoot me, but she was seriously unwell. What if, in a fit of rage, she pointed the gun at me and pulled the trigger before she could stop herself?

Mother pulled off the main road onto a bumpy side road. Not far away, the light from the drunken man's house glowed like the entrance to Hell.

Chapter Twenty-Nine

I'm going to die. I'm going to die.

I couldn't stop the four-word sentence rotating around my brain. It was because I had decided what to do when we reached the drunken man's farm. I had finally made a decision.

Mother slowed the car down, jiggled a stick in the middle of the car directly between us and yanked up another, straighter stick. The car jerked to a stop. The engine cut out. For a moment, we sat in the dark pool of the car, staring out at the light coming from the small house. The dogs in the cage had not barked. Neither had the dog chained to the building. Either they were asleep or they were not bothered by the car's arrival. I could hear her breathing. She sounded wheezy, out of breath despite the fact that we had been sat down for a while now.

"She's in there?"

Her question sent a shiver down my spine. Her voice was so cold and calculating. She had lost something and she wanted it back. Were Emma and I people to her or were we objects? She called us dolls. I had never thought how strange that was until recently, but a real mother with real love would never call her child a doll. A doll was dead. I was alive. Emma was alive. We could hurt. We could bleed.

I will bleed.

Mother slapped me around the face. "Answer me!"

I stared at her through the gloom, glad that the darkness hid the tears in my eyes. "Yes. I left her here."

I held my breath, certain she would hear my lie. She reached out and I flinched away, thinking she was going to strike me again, but she stroked my hair back from my forehead, her touch gentle.

"You're a good doll. I'm sorry I hit you. I'm just anxious about Emma, that's all."

I wanted to scream - to yank her hand away from me and give her a taste of her own, vile medicine, but I couldn't move. I couldn't raise my hand to her. Instead, I stared at her lap. At the gun, which looked like a stiff, black snake in the darkness. I imagined myself snatching it off her lap, turning it around deftly and pointing it at her. I pictured her reaction: shock, dismay, anger. Pictured her running away...

It all played out so perfectly and I began to believe I could do it. I could beat her. I could win. I could regain my freedom, save Emma, save Patrick, live a normal, happy life.

She grabbed my chin. "If you try to leave, you know what I'll do."

She opened the door and got out of the car without another word. I gawked at the car door as it banged shut. She had taken the gun with her. I scrabbled with my door handle, but the door was locked. I tried her door, the two back doors: all were locked.

Mother marched up to the house and banged on the door with

her fist. In her free hand she held the gun down by her side. She didn't even try to hide the weapon. She glanced back, her eyes warning me. I watched, fearful for the drunken man even though he was a pig. He didn't have a clue about Emma's whereabouts.

When there was no answer, she smashed the door again. Five times, louder than before. She waited, foot tapping the ground. After only a short wait, she raised the gun and smashed the door with the thick end. The door held despite her efforts, so she aimed the gun at the door and fired. The explosion made the car windows vibrate. If the drunken man was asleep before, he had to be awake now. Mother staggered back, reeling from the shock of the gun, dust and debris flying into her face. She coughed and dragged the back of her hand across her eyes. Without a backward glance, she kicked down the door and strode into the house.

I heard distant shouting. A man's and a woman's. I looked at the window beside my face then at the back seats. Mother's winter coat lay in the back. I grabbed it, wrapped it around my right elbow, turned to face the headrest and knelt up on the seat. Raising my elbow high, I pulled my arm back from the glass, gripping one fist in the other, took a deep breath and smashed my elbow as hard as I could into the passenger window. Pain ricocheted up my arm and I cried out. Breathing slowly and deeply, allowing the pain to ebb a little, I drew my arm up again, counted down from three then smashed my elbow into the glass again. This time a tiny crack the size of my thumb nail splintered the centre of the window. Fighting waves of pain and nausea, I turned around, wrapped the coat around my other elbow, gritted my teeth, closed my eyes and smashed my left elbow into the crack. Groaning with pain, I gritted my teeth and hit the window again, but it didn't shatter. I sank down onto my knees and hugged myself, breathing through the stabbing pains in my arms. My eyes fell on the door, on a handle of sorts. I grabbed the plastic handle and pushed it down and around; the window slid down a notch. My heart leapt and I turned the handle again, unwinding the window some more. I turned faster, unwinding the window as far as it would go. I unravelled the coat from my elbow and threw it onto the driver's seat. Stealing a glance at the broken front door of the house, I crawled through the window head first, the top of the window digging into my stomach. Stretching out my arms to the ground, I wriggled forward, lowering my upper body and performing a handstand of sorts in my effort to extricate the rest of my body from the car.

I pushed myself to my feet - and froze at Mother's voice. "Mirabelle, stop."

I turned. Mother pushed the drunken man to his knees in front of her. He looked at me through swollen, bruised eyes. Blood poured out of his nostrils onto his stained vest. He swayed on his knees then violently threw up onto his own lap. The stink of vomit hit the air.

"You saw this girl," Mother said, waving the gun at me, "and another one. A smaller girl. Emma. Where is she now? What have you done with her?"

She pointed the gun at the back of his head. His eyes rolled. He groaned and wiped his mouth with his hand.

"Tell me, Derek, or I'll put a fucking bullet in your thick head."

Derek tried to turn round to look at her and she kicked him hard in the back sending him forward onto all fours. He grunted and shook his head. Saliva dripped from his mouth onto the dirt. With difficulty he pushed himself back up onto his knees.

"Please don't hurt me, Mrs," he slurred, "I've got a kid."

"Tell me about Emma."

There was nothing I could do but stand there and watch. Derek seemed to be trying to find the right words. He frowned and wiped his nose, smearing blood across his cheek. Tears dripped down his cheeks.

"I don't know no Emma."

"The little girl *she* left here a few hours ago. You know exactly who I'm talking about. Tell me or I *will* shoot you."

Derek dropped his head and closed his eyes. He went very still and for a terrifying moment I thought he was dead, thought fear had killed him. Stopped his heart. Then his whole body jerked and he threw up again.

The air swelled with the sickly-sweet scent of vomit. My insides recoiled and I glanced at Mother, whose face twisted with disgust. She looked, in that moment in the dimly lit yard, like what I imagined a scarecrow to look like. Her straw-coloured hair stuck out at disturbing angles, her dark eyes stared blankly, unseeingly, and her skeletal body looked like it had been frozen in time. For too long she stood there unmoving, unblinking, the silence stretching on and up into the eternity of the space above our heads, into the stars, beyond the stars. She was all-powerful in that moment. She was God. Derek and I were nothing. She abruptly tilted her head to the side. Her eyes caught the light from the house and glinted. She smiled a smile that did not meet her eyes and then she shot a bullet into Derek's head.

I didn't scream. I was too shocked to scream or move or breathe. I stared as Derek's face exploded into a million pieces and his body dropped to the ground like a stone. I stared as Mother let the gun fall to the ground, marched over to me and seized my wrist. I stared as she dragged me to the car and shoved me in. Stared as she strapped the safety belt around me then got behind the wheel and started the car. Stared the whole drive back to the cottage, unable to think anything except for the same four words over and over and over again.

Chapter Thirty

Mother was a killer. She was completely insane. She'd shot Derek in the head and not even winced when she'd done it. She'd driven back to the cottage with the radio on, humming along to an upbeat song with a queer smile on her lips as though nothing had ever happened. As if Derek was still alive. As if both she and I weren't covered with his blood. As if we were a normal, happy mother and daughter going for a drive in the dark.

She hadn't said anything to me when we'd pulled up outside the cottage. She'd turned off the engine, exited the car, opened my door and lifted me out. I hadn't protested as she had carried me like a babe in arms into the cottage. Hadn't protested when she'd injected me with some kind of drug and put me in my bed and locked my bedroom door.

Morning had come and gone. I lay on my back in bed, head and limbs heavy. I stared at the ceiling, glanced at the door. She'd left the house about an hour ago.

The silence and gloom seemed to consume me. I lifted my arms, let them drop back onto the mattress. Everything felt so heavy, so difficult. Pointless.

Patrick needs your help.

There was that nagging voice again. From behind that voice came a stranger's voice. The voice was harsh and angry: *I never saw a wild thing sorry for itself. A small bird will drop frozen dead from a bough without ever having felt sorry for itself.*

I said the words out loud, testing them on my tongue. Then I screamed Patrick's name as loudly as I could and listened. There was no response. How long had it been since Mother had stabbed him? I couldn't work it out. The mathematical part of my brain seemed to be wading through the drugs, unable to perform as well as normal. I shouted his name again and again and again, listening in between each call and hearing nothing in return. I pushed myself out of bed and gingerly swivelled around to touch the floor with my bandaged feet. My entire body ached. I stood up and walked to the door, tested it just in case. It was locked. Of course it was. She would be more careful from now on. Now that she knew I could not be trusted. Perfect, obedient Mirabelle was gone, replaced by rebellious Polly Dalton. In Mother's books, I was untrustworthy and delusional, but she was the mentally unstable one. She was the killer.

A shiver trickled across my shoulders. I forced my thoughts away from Derek's headless body onto the here and now. If Patrick was still alive I could not just sit here and do nothing. Mother was out. This was my chance.

I turned my back to the locked door and surveyed the small room, looking at it with new eyes. I had no tools with which to prise the wooden boards from the windows and no weapon of any obvious kind. I walked over to my desk. A small black pot held my pens and pencils, a sharpener and a ruler. I picked up a pen, made a stabbing motion with it. I imagined stabbing Mother and my insides squirmed.

Despite the warmth of the room, cold chilled my bones. I pulled off the blood-stained brown dress and changed into a black doll dress with scarlet roses embroidered over the chest. I hated to wear one of her doll dresses again, but I had to get away from the blood stains.

The dress was so tight that I could barely draw breath, so I reached up behind my neck and ripped a tear down the back of the dress. The tearing sound was intensely satisfying. I stood in front of the mirror and craned my head round to look at the damage I had done to the back of the dress. Mother would be mad, but if things went my way, she would have little chance to react to what I'd done. I pulled on a fresh pair of knickers and a pair of black tights that I found in the back of the wardrobe. My body grew warm. Panic fluttered in my chest as I turned my attention back to the pot of pens and pencils.

I sat down at the desk and began to write a letter to my real parents, Jane and Peter Dalton. I wrote the word 'Dear' then paused, unsure what to call them. They were my mother and father, but it seemed odd to use those words. It seemed too familiar, yet they were my family. They were my real mother and father. I thought about the police. They would probably be first to find the letter, which meant I had to make it very clear who the letter was addressed to. I scrunched up the paper and grabbed a fresh sheet. This time I began 'Dear Jane and Peter'. Tears filled my eyes. I told myself not to over-think the words. Told myself to be honest and open and as factual as possible – keep my emotions out of it. If they ever read this letter, I would be dead, so they would have enough to deal with without me pouring out every little bad thing that had ever happened to me.

I wrote for two hours straight. Wrote until I heard the car pull up to the cottage.

I folded the letter up and tucked it down inside my tights, wrapping it around the bandage on my right foot.

She was back.

I grabbed my fountain pen, lay down on the bed and dug my teeth into my left wrist, tasting blood.

Chapter Thirty-One

I heard rather than saw Mother open the door. She stepped into the room. The door creaked and knocked against the wall.

Mother didn't move toward the bed. I caught a faint whiff of orange-blossom moisturiser.

"Mirabelle?" her voice was quiet.

I didn't move, didn't flinch when she took a step forward. I kept my eyes closed and focused on listening to her movements.

"Mirabelle?"

I tried to breathe with as little chest movement as possible. She took another step closer and a small cry burst from her lips. She mumbled something about blood. So much blood. She was crying. She was crying for me. My resolve wavered. I reminded myself what she had done to Patrick, Dot and Derek. How she had kidnapped Emma and me. How she would never stop unless someone made her stop.

Something clattered to the floor and I jumped. Keys. She had dropped her keys.

"Mirabelle? Mirabelle!"

She rushed forward suddenly. I opened my eyes and sat up as she bent over me. Bringing my right hand over her arched back, I stabbed the fountain pen into her left shoulder. She screamed. Her eyes widened and she grabbed at me as I tried to crawl past her. I fell to the floor and she seized my ankle and dragged me backward as I fought to claw forward. I kicked out and caught her in the face. She roared but released my foot, and I pushed myself up and ran out of the room.

I flew down the stairs and tried the front door, which was locked. I ran into the kitchen. Patrick's body was gone. The floor was clean too. I opened a drawer, but hands seized me from behind. I cried out and tried to twist out of Mother's grasp as she threw me into the kitchen table. My stomach smashed against wood, and fire exploded in my stomach. I dropped to my knees and tried to crawl away, blinded by tears of pain, not knowing which way I was headed.

Mother grabbed a handful of my hair and pulled me to my feet. She yanked my head back, exposing my throat and smiled down at me. Blood soaked her blouse and the end of her hair.

"You conniving bitch," she spat.

She seized the wrist that I'd bitten and looked at it then threw my hand away and shook her head bitterly.

"You're nothing to me anymore. I've given you chance after chance and now this..."

She yanked out a chair and shoved me onto the wooden seat.

"Don't move," she said, nostrils flaring.

She opened a drawer and pulled out a knife. Turning around, she glared at me. She sat down opposite me and lunged forward, positioning the knife behind my right ear.

"What do you do with a broken doll?" she said, tilting her head. Her eyes looked black. They had taken on that faraway look.

I didn't move. I stared at the table. Shakes overtook my body; I shook so violently that the table vibrated.

Silent tears ran down her cheeks and she looked at me with something like pity. "Don't worry. I'm not going to kill you. I'm going to give you what you've always wanted."

Hope flickered in my chest and I glanced up at her.

She smiled. "I'm going to let you go outside. You'd like that wouldn't you?"

All hope vanished. She was smiling the smile that didn't meet her eyes and it struck me that she was enjoying herself. She smoothed back my hair from my face. I flinched but she didn't seem to notice.

"Get up," she said softly.

I did as she said, watching the knife, which she moved out of the way to allow me space to stand. She stood too, grabbed my hand and pulled me toward the back door.

The door was unlocked. She opened it and we walked out together, hand in hand. The day was overcast and muggy. I stared at trees and overgrown grass and mottled, grey sky as she pulled me round to the back of the cottage.

"This is the back garden you've always wanted to see," she said, gesturing with the knife to a jungle with a large brown square in the centre.

"My grandfather spent many hours out here, you know," she said dreamily, "he made me and Sarah come out here a lot too."

We walked forward into the overgrown garden. The grass was as tall as my waist and so bright it made my eyes sting. Enclosing the garden was a dilapidated fence and beyond the fence stood the woods.

"We spent a lot of time out here as children, you know," she said.

She stopped and stared down at the brown square on the ground. I followed her gaze and frowned, confused. The brown square looked like two rusted, metal doors. Two doors *in the ground*.

Mother pushed me onto my front on top of the door. She knelt down, resting one knee on my back to keep me still. Holding the knife between her teeth, she pulled a key out of her pocket and unlocked the door.

I suddenly realised what she was going to do. I struggled to get up but she crushed me against the ground with her knee.

"I'm only giving you what you've always wanted," she said in a sing-song voice.

She flung open one of the doors and a foetid stench filled the air. She seized my shoulders and pulled me onto her lap, holding the knife to my cheek. I stared down at the hole in the ground, unable to believe what was happening.

"Be a good girl and you'll get all the food and water you need," she whispered.

"No! Please – don't!" I screamed and swivelled round, pleading, begging her with my eyes.

With a distant smile she pushed me off her lap. I rolled through the doorway down some steps. Above me the door slammed, and I was swallowed by darkness.

Chapter Thirty-Two

It was the kind of blackness where it was impossible to see anything, even the faintest hint of your own hand an inch from your face. I had known darkness but never darkness this thick. Like tar. Like a demon's blood. I lifted my hand and held it in front of my face. Nothing. Just black. Black and an awful smell. A smell so revolting that I retched continuously for about five minutes. I could not be sick and add to this smell. It was the smell of dirt and decay. The smell of grime and poo and urine and mould and rot all rolled into one gut-wrenchingly hideous stench.

I sat up and felt the step around me. It was made of bricks. Dust or sand or dry crumbs of soil lay on the brick surface. Steps meant man-made, which meant this was not a simple hole in the ground. This hole was more than that. But what was it? Why would someone dig a hole in the ground, build steps leading down into the earth and place doors on top? 'The Wizard of Oz' jumped into my head. When the tornado had struck, the characters had hidden in the ground. Perhaps this hole was like that. A place to escape terrible weather. But I had never known weather bad enough to destroy a house. England didn't have tornadoes. I would have heard such a crazy gale, even through the wooden boards that blocked every window in the cottage.

So what was it? And why did it carry such a gross stench?

If I could understand what kind of place I was in, maybe I could find a way out.

Stretching out one foot, I felt the ground in front of me. It was another step. I slid onto it, staying on my bottom. I slid down another three steps until I felt hard, solid ground. To my surprise, the ground was smooth, like plastic. Another clue, yet I still couldn't work out what type of prison held me its prisoner. Fearful of bumping into something, I got down on all fours and edged forward an inch at a time, feeling the ground with my hands. Every few inches I stopped and gingerly felt the air around me, searching for more clues.

My stomach grumbled. I hadn't eaten anything since the sandwich Dot had given me. My heart began to race; what if Mother forgot to bring me something to eat and drink? I hadn't drunken anything for ages either.

Telling myself she would remember, I crawled on, feeling the ground. I felt brick. My hands moved upward, trailing up a solid, brick wall. I rose to my knees and reached up. The wall continued upward. I stood up slowly, worried I might hit my head if the ceiling was too low, but I was able to stand up straight. I felt for the ceiling, but couldn't reach it. The hole was deep.

Relieved to be able to stand up straight, I moved to the right and reached another brick wall, which I followed round until I reached the steps that led down here. I retraced my steps, moving back round to the left, hands trailing the brick wall. My feet collided with something hard and I jumped at the unexpected object. It was a bookcase. I felt the spines of books, my heart lifting a notch. If I could persuade Mother to bring me a light of some kind at least I could read until I could work out a way to escape.

I didn't let myself consider the possibility of never escaping. I told myself that Mother would let me out eventually or I would escape. I would get out of here, one way or another. I had to.

Emma's big eyes flashed into my mind. Emma was still out there somewhere. Hot shame swept over me. It was my fault she was out there all alone. Mother would never have put Emma down here. If I had helped her find Emma, Emma would be safe and sound in the cottage – as safe as she could be with a kidnapper...

I closed my eyes, forced myself to focus on now. Focus on where I was, what I was doing.

The air was warm and thick. Too warm. I yanked on the collar of the stupid doll dress and blew air down my front, but my breath was hot and did little to cool my skin.

Tears welled up, but I gritted my teeth, determined not to give up.

I edged past the bookcase and felt the wall again. Nothing. I side-stepped to the left, trailing my fingers across the bricks. My hands bumped into something else – something metal that rose as high as my waist. I moved my hands from the wall to the metal object and quickly worked out that it was a metal bed frame. Bending over, I felt bed covers, a mattress and a sheet. There was a single bed down here. At least if Mother did leave me here for a while, I would have somewhere to sleep. A dirty bed was better than a dirty floor.

I felt my way to the end of the bed and my hands landed on a thin pillow. Kneeling down, I tentatively felt under the bed, but there was nothing there except for dust and grime. Wiping my hands on my dress, I stood up and turned. Again, I felt brick wall and trailed my hands along the rough surface as I inched to the left. I bumped into a small table. There were no chairs near the table and nothing on the table.

Using the table top as a guide, I edged round the table then found wall again. The brick wall changed texture and I realised I was touching a wooden door. Hurriedly, thinking I'd found an escape route, I felt for a handle. Finding one, I pushed down and pulled. Pulling didn't work so I pushed the door open. I gagged as the stench increased tenfold. Still, I edged forward and felt around myself. My hands touched brick wall on either side and my leg collided with something hard. I was in a tiny room. I reached down, my fingertips outstretched. My fingers touched a brick table of some kind. I trailed my fingers along its surface and they fell into a hole in the brick. This was where the stench was strongest. A fly buzzed around my head. Another fly landed on my hand.

Unable to bear the smell any longer, I turned around and shuffled back toward the door using the side walls as my guide. I reached the doorway, hurried through, turned and grappled for the handle, pulling the door shut, desperate to put a barrier between myself and the stench.

So the small room was a bathroom of some kind. My whole body jolted. If the bathroom smelt that bad, the stench so fresh...someone was using it.

I leaned against the wall, the wind knocked out of me.

I wasn't alone.

A stranger was down here with me.

Chapter Thirty-Three

In the impenetrable darkness I stood still and listened. Listened for the sound of someone's breathing. If I was right, and I was sure I was, a stranger was sitting in the darkness listening to my movements. This stranger must have heard me. They must have heard Mother push me down here. They must have heard me tumbling down the steps, getting up, moving around the space like a blind girl. This stranger had listened to my terror and said nothing. Why? Were they too afraid to make themselves known? Did this stranger expect to remain unknown to me – was that what he or she wanted? Did they want to attack me, take me by surprise?

Scenarios whizzed around my head like bees in a box, my imagination frantic. Spiders were down here – huge ones – spiders with huge fangs and eight beady eyes and a savage lust for human blood. And rats. There were bound to be lots of rats. Rats were attracted to foul, reeking places and this place reeked. And the stranger – the stranger would be worse than Mother. They would be rabid with hunger. To them I would be nothing more than a way to keep themselves fed.

My hands found my head. My temples throbbed against my palms. Dizziness danced behind my eyes. My stomach rippled with anxiety.

Stop it. Think. A wild bird never feels sorry for itself.

I listened hard. I could almost picture my ears perking up, twitching at the ends. But I heard nothing. The silence was as contained and absolute as the dark. All-encompassing. I remembered a day Mother and I had played hide and seek. We had laughed and chased one another. Mother had caught me and tickled me. There had been few days like that. Few moments when Mother had relaxed and let me behave naturally, but those moments had been the best....and now she had locked me in a hole in the ground in complete darkness with a stranger. Had this always been coming? Would things have stayed the same forever if Mother had never taken Emma or would she have taken another girl later on? Was I going to die down here?

A wild bird never feels sorry for itself.

I took a deep breath. Counted to ten. My breathing slowed.

If she wanted me dead, she would have killed me instead of putting me down here. And if the stranger wanted to hurt me, they would have acted by now.

Time stood still. I opened my mouth to speak then shut it again. If I was quiet and hid, I would be safer - unless the stranger was some kind of supernatural creature – which of course they couldn't be - they were as blind as I was down here, which meant silence was my weapon.

Mentally, I retraced my path, recalling the table I had bumped into. I wanted to get back to the bed. The space underneath had been wide enough for me to fit. If I could hide there, I could wait him or her out. They might even give themselves away if the need to cough or sneeze suddenly became too much.

Using the wall for guidance, I turned around and inched back the way I had come. Trying not to think of spiders or rats or the stranger in the room, my fingertips scraped brick and I hoped, even as I tried not to think about them, that any spiders or dungeon-type insects would feel my fingers coming and dart out of the way.

Sweat trickled down the side of my face as I eased myself around the table and edged in the direction of the bed. I closed my eyes against the blackness and willed myself to believe it was black because of my choosing. I had *chosen* to rest my eyes, to submerge myself in inky darkness. I needed to give my eyes a break – they had been dazzled by the sun and they needed a break...

But I could feel a strange heaviness dragging down the space behind my eyes. Blinds were being pulled down. Boards were being nailed over the gap between the backs of my eyes and my brain. It was such a strange, overwhelming sensation that I opened my eyes and almost gasped. How long had I been down here? I couldn't work it out. An hour? Five hours? Or was it only minutes? Panic made my insides crawl and my breaths grow ragged.

Trembling, I silently repeated my mantra over and over as I edged, inch by inch, toward my goal.

A wild bird never feels sorry for itself. A wild bird never feels sorry for itself.

Then I realised the blind stupidity of what I was saying: I was not a wild bird; I was a caged one. I was not free.

My leg hit the bed and I almost cried out. Hastily, feeling like it was the only thing that would save me, I got to my knees and felt the bed frame with my hands then the space between the frame and the floor. Yes. I would fit. I would definitely fit.

I lay down on my front, turned onto my back and shuffled sideways under the bed, cursing the faint scraping of fabric against ground.

I had moved about three inches into the space when I smelt something odd. A different smell. A smell like bad breath.

And then I heard it. Breathing. Low, ragged breathing. Breathing that wasn't mine.

A hand squeezed my arm, and I screamed.

Chapter Thirty-Four

"It steals from you. Takes from your soul."

The voice was harsh. Fast. A woman's voice. A voice that produced hot fumes of the foulest kind.

I pursed my lips together and held my breath. Our faces could not have been more than an inch apart. If she wanted to she could bite off my nose or push her fingers deep into my eye sockets, into my brain. She could kill me in a heartbeat if she chose to.

Her fingers dug into my arm, holding on too tightly - so tightly I wanted to ask her to let go, but I didn't. I couldn't breathe, couldn't speak; I ought to have been relieved the stranger was female, but I wasn't. The craziest person I knew was a woman; a woman had shut me down here in the dark; kidnapped me and Emma; shot a man in the head. A woman I had known for most of my life had rejected me, turned on me, locked me in a black hole in the ground. If Mother could treat me like that, what could this woman do to me?

"I see things. Lights. In the corners. Lights in the corners," she sounded rushed, like she had to get the words out or they would choke her.

"Then blackness. Nothing else. Just a tunnel. Are you really here? Are you?"

Her hand clenched, squeezed tighter, dug in to my skin and she began to shake my arm. My heart felt like it was going to explode out of my chest. I tried to pull my arm out of her grasp, but she clung on, grabbing at my chest, my face, my hair.

"Are you real? Speak! Speak to me!"

"Stop!" I blurted as she shook harder.

Abruptly, taking me by surprise, her hands stilled. One hand still gripped my arm while the other lay flat against my cheek.

"Say something," she whispered.

I hesitated, took a breath. "Let go of me."

I waited, tense, readying myself for another attack. Her breaths were ragged, louder than mine. A bark of laughter escaped her lips and spittle landed on my cheek. She patted my chest then removed her hand from my pounding heart. Her other hand loosened on my arm, but remained in contact with my skin. With one hot finger, she stroked my arm. I longed to move out of reach but feared what she might do if I moved suddenly.

"Are you *really* real?" she breathed.

"Yes." *The sounds I'd heard from the house. They came from here. From her. I hadn't imagined them.*

"Hah! Prove it."

"What?" I said, "How? I'm already talking to you, aren't I? And you can feel me, can't you? You can probably even smell me."

She didn't say anything for a long time - just breathed against my cheek and stroked my arm, drawing a figure of eight on my skin with her finger. It was creepy and weird but kind of soothing at the same time. I listened to her breaths grow steadier and felt my own heartbeat slowing.

After a while, she stopped stroking me and removed her hand from my arm. Her breathing quietened and for a few seconds, I thought she was dead.

"Miss?" I said, "Are you okay?"

She began to cry, quietly at first, then loudly and wretchedly. Beside me, I could feel her body shaking. Her sobs swallowed me whole. She sounded so lost and hopeless that I felt for her hand in the dark and slipped my hand into hers.

"You're not alone anymore," I said, "I'm real. I promise."

She allowed me to hold her hand, though hers was floppy in mine. She sniffed and cried, sniffed and cried. For a long time, I said nothing. Sometimes it was good to cry. I tried to think of a word that meant letting out all of your emotions, but my mind felt heavy and blank, as blank as the darkness around us. I stared into the black air. After a while, her hand responded in mine.

"Thank you," she said softly.

"Come on," I said, "Let's get out from under here. You can lie on the bed and rest."

"Yes, yes. You're probably right."

I slipped my hand out of hers and shuffled my body out from under the bed. Glad to be off the hard ground, I stepped back to give her enough space then felt for the bed frame and guided her onto the mattress. Through the thin material of her clothing I felt a hard, bony rod on her back, which I assumed was her spine. I couldn't help wonder if she had always been so skinny or if being down here had turned her into a skeleton. Had Mother been starving her? Would she starve me too? Mother had said that if I was good, she would bring me food and water. Had she said that to the lady too?

"I need to sleep," she said, her voice thick from crying.

I nodded, then realised I had to speak or she wouldn't have a clue about my response.

"Of course. Lie down and have a rest. I'll sit on the edge of the bed, if that's okay?"

"Tell me again," she said.

"What?"

"Tell me you're real."

I swallowed, mouth dry. How long had she been down here all alone?

"Please," she said, "Tell me."

"I'm real. I promise. I'm real and my name's Polly."

"Polly...that's a nice name..."

I wanted to ask her a million questions but her breathing told me she was already asleep, so I sat on the bed in the pitch black and tried to take comfort in one fact: I was not alone.

Chapter Thirty-Five

My brain was black. Burnt toast. My eyes were black. Coals, soot, death. My body was black. Mother's eyes. Black was evil. A colour that murdered other colours. But it wasn't just a colour anymore. It was a killing force. A force that murdered hope – stole from you. I knew what she meant now. Knew something - however small - of what she'd suffered.

Open-eyed I stared into the nothingness that was somehow all there was, and blackness rolled over me like an incessant swell of cold, pitiless waves; swallowed me whole like a shark gorging on a shoal of fish. I was trapped inside a belly of black where tar-like acid oozed down the walls and flooded the void. Darkness. Black. Too much black.

ABBA played in my head. Over and over again the same tinny lyrics rotated, providing an eerily jolly background to my morbid thoughts. With every passing second, my body seemed to float away from my mind, and the only thing that stopped me believing it gone was the hard mattress beneath me. If not for that blessed slab, I would have begun to believe that I only existed as a mind.

I fought to recapture images of the woods and the fields, the greenness, but black was a fierce foe. A thief. A murderer. Like Mother. She was the reason I was here. She needed to...

"Who's there!" The woman's voice cut in. Shrill. Afraid.

"Me. Polly," I said quickly, startled into a response.

"Polly? Oh yes...I remember. I'm sorry. Your voice startled me awake."

"My voice?" *Had I been speaking? Saying my thoughts out loud?*

"You were talking really fast. Saying the word 'black' a lot."

I heard the mattress springs squeal as she shifted her weight, and suddenly felt dizzy with relief. She was awake. Together. We could get through this together.

"I'm glad you're awake," I said, tearful all of a sudden.

She laughed softly, but there was no humour in it. "I'm glad you're still here. For a moment I thought I'd dreamt you."

"How long, "I hesitated, frightened by what she might say, "How long have you been down here?"

"I don't know."

"You don't...know? But, how can that be?"

"Time slips away here. There's no sense of morning and night. Minutes feels like hours. I sleep a lot, but I never feel rested."

I swallowed a lump of mucus. It slithered reluctantly down my throat. "I'm so sorry. I can't imagine what you've been through. What you're still going through."

She didn't say anything, so I gave her time. I shifted my weight. Numbness had started to creep in.

"How old are you, Polly?"

"Thirteen."

"Fuck."

I jumped at the curse.

"Sorry," she said.

"It's fine. Fuck," I said, testing the word. It felt good somehow, "Fuck, fuck, fuck!"

She laughed. This time her laugh sounded more real.

"FUCK!" she shouted.

"FUCK!" I shouted back.

We giggled. After a short while, we fell silent.

"Will you hold my hand?" I said.

"Of course I will."

Our fingers found each other's and we held hands in the darkness, silent for a time.

"I've never said a swearword before," I said.

"I hadn't when I was your age. I've said a lot since then though. Sometimes I scream and curse until my throat's raw."

"How old are you?" I said.

"I was thirty-two when she put me down here."

Her answer reminded me that she had no idea how long she'd been held captive. It was a horrifying thought. Would I still be here when I was twenty? Twenty-five? Thirty-two? Would Mother really do that to me? I couldn't bear to think about it.

Her stomach grumbled. I rested my free hand on my own hollow stomach.

"When did you last have something to eat?" I said, fear trickling down my spine.

She sighed. "I don't know. Sometimes I think she's trying to starve me to death - then she'll open the roof and put a cup of water and a sandwich on the step."

"Does she ever talk to you?"

"No. At first I tried to reason with her, but I don't bother anymore. She's a cold-hearted bitch. Totally insane."

"Have you ever tried -"

"Escape? Yes. And I nearly died in the process."

"What happened?"

"I must have been here less than a week. I spent my time working out where everything was. Feeling for anything I could use as a weapon, but there was nothing except for a small table. Back then I was still strong enough to lift it above my head – but only just. I hadn't eaten anything for days by that point and hunger was making me weak.

"I positioned the table on my lap and sat at the top of the stairs for God knows how long, waiting for her to come. I didn't even know for sure that she would come. I was terrified that she was going to leave me here, let me starve.

"But finally she came. I heard scraping above my head so I grabbed the table and the moment she opened the roof fully – because that's what she used to do - I threw the table as hard as I could through the opening, straight at her.

"But her reactions were too quick – she threw out her hands sending the table back into my face. The force sent me tumbling down the steps. I landed awkwardly – *really* awkwardly - and for a while I didn't dare move, thinking I'd broken my neck. She slammed the roof shut, leaving me nothing but a cup of water.

"I lay there sobbing. I was in agony and too scared to move. After a long time, I got up the courage and managed to pull myself up to a sitting position. My neck was very sore but not broken.

"She didn't bring me any food for a really long time. I thought I was going to starve to death. Since then I've thought about trying something again, but I'm so weak and I keep having visions of breaking my neck for real."

"Fuck," I said.

"Yeah. Fuck."

"Did she say anything when she brought you food?" I said.

"Kind of. Before she opened the roof she shouted in that she was holding a knife and that if I tried anything, she'd stab me to death then leave me down here to the rats."

"Rats?" I said, a sick feeling crawling up my throat.

"Yeah. They mostly leave you alone. It's only if you've got an open sore that they come sniffing around. They freaked me out at first, but I'm used to them now."

Rats. Sneaky, hairy, dirty rats. Rats with sharp, yellow teeth and evil, blood-red eyes.

I shivered. Thought about the cut on my wrist. The blood was congealed now. Did that mean the rats would not be interested or would they still be drawn by the lingering scent of relatively fresh blood?

She must have felt my reaction because she said, "Don't worry Polly. Honestly, you're a lot bigger and scarier to them than they are to you."

Something soothing about the way she spoke made me wonder if she had children. I opened my mouth to ask, then stopped. If she did have children, what had happened to them? They might have been left alone in their home with no-one to care for them. They could have starved to death by now – or maybe Mother had done something to them too. Bringing up the subject didn't seem a sensible thing to do. Not yet anyway. I resolved not to mention the subject yet.

"Tell me if you don't want to talk about it, okay," she said, "but I can't help wanting to know why *you're* down here?"

She asked the question as if she knew why she was down here. Curiosity got the better of me and I blurted, "Why are *you* down here?"

She laughed – this time a bitter, hard sound. "Because she's mad. She's always been mad."

"*Always* been mad? What do you mean? Have you known her for a long time?"

She didn't reply.

Icy fingers of dread unfurled across the back of my neck. "Your name's Sarah, isn't it?"

"Yes - how on earth do you know that?"

I took a deep breath, unable to believe it.

"Polly? How do you know my name?" Her voice rushed out of her, urgent and panicky. She let go of my hand and moved closer to me on the bed.

"I, er, it's a long story," I said.

"Tell me," she urged, finding my shoulders in the dark, her fingers a little too tight as they gripped me, "Tell me everything."

Chapter Thirty-Six

I told her everything, just as she'd asked. As I talked I was surprised to hear hollowness in my voice, but Sarah made interested noises. Occasionally she gasped or groaned or rubbed my shoulders, while I twisted my hands together in the darkness, glad to be invisible as I silently strove to slow the storming of my heart – a violent wildness that betrayed my calm facade. Dredging up the past ten years was like inflicting scolding hot lashes on my own back. Oh why did she have to choose me, choose anyone?

As the years had mounted, so had Mother's madness; as I had matured, so too had her shift toward insanity. Or had it? Maybe she had managed to hide her craziness from me in the early days – or maybe I had been too young and naïve to notice the signs. Her threat to make my imaginary friend, Polly, go away, for example, if I didn't rid myself of Polly...what human would do that to a child? Threaten them over such a silly yet comforting choice that was ultimately theirs to make? What harm did it do? But I knew the answer to that now. *I* was Polly and Mother hadn't wanted me to remember that important fact. So there was a reason to her madness, in a way. A reason that supported her belief that kidnapping another person's child was perfectly acceptable.

Through Sarah's reactions and my narration of events past, I now saw that I'd been looking at Mother through the rose-tinted glasses of youth. I had been fragile, innocent and all-too-willing to believe in her lies. Intoxicated by her obsession with me, I'd wanted to trust her because I'd needed her. She had, after all, been my only parental figure and at times she'd given me some semblance of a normal childhood. She had not been horrible to me all of the time. Sometimes, especially when I was little, she had played with me, baked cakes with me, read to me at bedtime...

"You're being too generous," Sarah said.

"What do you mean?"

"You're trying to make excuses for her. Trying to understand her. She told you that you were allergic to light, for Christ's sakes! She stopped you from going outside! And now she's locked you in a hole in the ground!"

"I know..." I trailed off, knowing she was right, but not knowing why I felt the need to rationalise Mother's behaviour.

"She's stone cold crazy, believe me. *I* know - she's always been crazy."

I said nothing. I didn't want to force Sarah to tell me.

Silence flooded the space between us, and my eyes grew heavier and heavier. The darkness pressed down and an irresistible sleepiness teased my mind. Silence reigned for a long time. I began to drift away.

"She's my sister," Sarah murmured, "My twin sister."

I jerked upright, eyes wide, suddenly alert. Had Sarah ever told anyone about her childhood? If this was the first time, it would be difficult for her, maybe impossible. But I wanted to know everything. I wanted to understand *her*. Mother. Understand how she could bring herself to do the terrible things she had done.

Sarah sighed heavily. "Four. We were four when I started noticing something off about Katherine."

"Off?" *Katherine. So that's her name.*

"Yes. Strange. Disturbing. My earliest memory is her twisting the head off a doll then stamping on its face. I think she was mad because she'd been told off. I don't remember the details. She always had a terrible temper.

"Anyway. We didn't get on like twins are supposed to. Katherine hated me. I started to feel it when we were probably around six or seven years old. I'd sense her glaring at me from across the room as I sat on the old bastard's lap. Part of it, I think, was jealousy. I was prettier than Katherine and people commented on it all the time. And the old bastard - almost every day he'd admire me – in front of her. He'd dress us in these ridiculous dresses that looked like something out of a fairytale, then stand back and say how I looked like an angel. *His* angel. I suppose I should have picked up the warning signs then, but I was too innocent to believe that adults could be so evil."

"Did you and Katherine go to school?" I said, prompting her to continue.

"We did, for a while."

"What was she like – at school, I mean?"

Sarah laughed humourlessly. "Worse than at home."

"How?"

"She stole every friend I ever made. Spread nasty rumours about me. Got me in trouble with the teachers. It sounds pretty petty stuff now but at the time it made my life hell. I couldn't get anyone to play with me at break or lunchtimes so I made friends with a black cat called Sooty who prowled around the playground every day. He was the most affectionate cat you'll ever meet. He used to follow me around every day. Being with Sooty made me feel a little less lonely, I think."

I could sense a 'but' coming and held my breath.

"Then that nasty little bitch decided to take him away from me too."

"No – what did she do?"

Horrid ideas stormed around my mind – she'd kicked the cat so it had never come back – or she'd thrown rocks at it and scared it away – or -

"She put him in a bin and set the bin on fire. I'll never forget the sound. Or the smell."

I felt sick.

"How, how old was she when she did it?"

"Nine."

"Did anyone find out she did it?"

Another bitter laugh. "She tried to pin it on me, but luckily another child saw her do it. She got expelled. The next three years were the best of my life because I went to school without her and actually made some friends."

"Did he find out?"

"Yes. He shut her down here for five days. At the time I thought she deserved worse than that but now..."

"What was she like when he let her out?"

Sarah went quiet for a moment. I could tell she was thinking.

She sighed. "She was quieter. A lot quieter come to think of it. And she tried her hardest to please him any way she could. I'd still catch her staring daggers at me but she spent most of her time –

when I was around anyway – with her head in a book."

"Did he home-school her?"

"Yes. I think he only taught her Maths and English though."

"You said the next three years were the best of your life – why only three -" Then I remembered. My mouth snapped shut.

Sarah seemed not to notice. She spoke with no emotion. "When I was twelve he started to abuse me, sexually. It went on for three years until I got pregnant and ran away."

"I'm sorry," I swallowed, not sure whether to ask my question or not.

"He never touched Katherine," she said, her voice turning hard, "She took photographs while he..."

I gasped, unable to hide my shock. "What? She - *photographs?*"

"Yes. Like I said. Stone cold crazy."

Chapter Thirty-Seven

We sat in silence holding hands.

I groped for words but could not find ones that would do. I longed to know what had happened to the baby, but didn't dare ask. If Sarah felt like telling me, she would.

My tummy roiled with hunger and emotion, and part of me wanted to close my eyes, go to sleep and forget everything she had just told me. Another part felt like tearing something to pieces, bashing my fists into the wall. Sarah had suffered so much cruelty and Mother had helped a lot of that cruelty along. There was no question in my mind that Mother was disturbed but there was also no question in my mind that she was evil too.

"Fuck," Sarah said, "I shouldn't have told you all that. You'll have nightmares for a month."

"No I won't. Don't worry about me. I want to know everything. I need to know."

"Thanks Polly."

"For what?"

"For listening. I've never told anyone about my childhood. Even when I had the abortion and the nurses treated me like shit, I never told what he'd done."

"You had an abortion?"

"Yes. I don't even feel guilty about it. Not when it was his."

I didn't know what to say so I said nothing. Blackness yawned in front of me and I shivered.

"I'm married now to a wonderful, funny man called Robert and we have twin boys, Andrew and David. They're three."

"What are they like? Your sons?"

"Lovely. A handful but lovely. Every time I think about them, my heart breaks."

"I can't imagine what you're going through. What date did she put you here?" I said, finding my nails in the dark and beginning to bite.

"March 5th."

"What year?"

"1976."

"It was 5th May 1976 when I tried to escape, which means you've been down here for..." My brain worked frantically, my teeth nibbled and tore, nibbled and tore, "sorry – my brain seems to have slowed down. I must have been put down here on the 7th or 8th May, which means you've been down here for sixty-three or sixty-four days. Gosh."

"Two months? Is that it?" she paused, "It's my little boys' fourth birthday next week," she said, so quietly I could barely hear.

"How – er – how did she find you? What happened?" I said, desperate to know but equally desperate to take her mind off her sons. She sounded like she was about to disintegrate.

Her voice trembled. She cleared her throat and sniffed. "I was stupid enough to come back here. I don't know why I did it. I think it was because I finally felt normal again. No-one told me to do it. I just came. I'd been thinking about doing it for a long time and it was a nice day for March. The boys were at their grandparents' and Robert was at work. Work finished early so I drove here. I only live an hour's drive away.

"I thought she was gone. All these years I had created this fantasy that she'd moved to France, like she used to say she would when he was out of earshot. I knew the old bastard was dead because a friend of his managed to track down my address and sent me a letter telling me about the funeral, which of course I didn't go to. I was glad he was dead. Ecstatic in fact. It felt like a huge weight had been lifted from my shoulders. I think knowing he was dead was what allowed me to open myself up to the idea of falling in love.

"Anyway, where was I? Oh yes. It's my bloody fault I'm here. My stupid idea to come back, face my fears."

"So you drove right up to the cottage?" I prompted, tasting blood from a torn cuticle.

"Yes. I noticed boards on the windows and thought some homeless person might have holed up inside. I didn't want to go in. I just wanted to see it; I don't know why – it's hard to explain.

"I got out of my car and wandered up to the front door. The same smells – smells of trees and grass and swamp and pollen – began to overwhelm me, and I started to cry. I couldn't be there. I knew I'd made a mistake – I wasn't ready. Would never be ready.

"So I turned to go and her car was pulling up behind mine, blocking me in. I froze. She got out of her car and we stared at each other. I was so surprised that I didn't speak. She looked so much older. Thinner, haggard, but those hateful eyes were the same.

"I found my voice and told her I was going. Could she move her car? She didn't reply; just walked towards me, her head tilted to the side, a strange smile on her face.

"I asked her again to move her car, but she ignored me and kept walking over. I asked her to move her car one more time. She didn't say anything, just smirked. I didn't know what to do. She slid her hand into her pocket then raised her hand. She was holding a knife.

"She said, 'I'm so happy you came back, Sis. It's so great to see you.' Her voice was flat, strange.

"I asked her what the knife was for but she said nothing. She stopped a yard from me and said, 'Your choice: shelter or knife.'

"I tried to run past her, but she grabbed my arm and whirled me in front of her, pressing the knife against my throat, cutting into my skin. She pushed me into the back garden, unlocked the doors and shoved me down here without a single match."

"I'm so sorry," I murmured, clutching her hand in the dark.

"You've nothing to be sorry for. I'm only sorry I ever came back. And I told no-one where I was going. I've hoped and prayed someone would find my car and track me here, but surely they would have found something by now."

"How's your neck now?" I said.

"It's fine. She only grazed me. It's the hunger that's killing me – and the dark – so much dark. It makes my mind do crazy things."

"I know," I said, "When you were asleep, I started losing my mind. I was *so* relieved when you woke up. I can't imagine how you've coped being alone down here all this time."

"My boys. And Robert. They're all that's kept me going. But I'm ashamed to admit I'd started thinking of ways to end it, then you came along. You've saved me, Polly. You really have. Just talking about everything is helping a little."

"We're getting out of here," I said, hearing hopelessness in her weak voice.

She said nothing. I could hear her stomach rumbling. The snip, snip, snip as she bit her nails too.

She was silent for a long time. We sat holding hands, both shaking with too many emotions to name.

Finally, she cleared her throat. "How? How are we getting out of here?"

I didn't reply. I didn't know what to say.

Chapter Thirty-Eight

Hunger and fear kept me awake but Sarah slept again. I listened to her long, slow breaths and brought my hand to my lips. My fingers trembled, my mouth felt like it had been dried out with toilet paper and my head banged. Each bang was the fist of someone trapped inside my skull desperate to get out. Each bang echoed the anger and fear that throbbed in my veins.

I was still running on adrenaline. I knew that and it terrified me. When that adrenaline ebbed, fear would beat anger back down into the dirt, and I needed the anger that thrummed in my chest like a bird's wings. Anger gave me courage. Anger was good.

Before my anger could dwindle, I had to work out how this would play out, but Mother was so unpredictable there seemed too many ways this could go. I closed my eyes and pictured her face, trying to put myself in her position, think how she thought, see the world and Sarah and me through Mother's eyes. Sarah said that their grandfather had never sexually abused Mother, but he had locked her down here, which was a cruel punishment that she had gone on to use herself on Sarah and then me. That was behaviour she had learnt and copied. From what Sarah had told me, I got the impression that their grandfather had been a cold, unloving man – traits that Mother also possessed, but Mother could also be caring. She liked to nurture little girls into her vision of the perfect doll; pretty, immaculately put-together, flawless. She liked her dolls to be obedient, quiet and docile. And young. Dolls were only perfect when they were undeveloped. That was why I was out. I was turning into a woman and Mother couldn't handle that – but why? Why did my physical development and biological progress disturb her so much? If I could solve that puzzle, maybe I could work out how to convince her to let us out. That was if she ever came back with the food and water she'd promised...she might decide to let us both starve to death.

I shivered, and shivered again. The dank, moist air was deep in my bones. Though the space was warm, so warm and muggy that I felt like I was inhaling steam, a tepid dampness had tunnelled itself into my flesh.

My stomach was already beginning to eat itself and I had not been down here for very long at all. It seemed impossible that Sarah had survived this long. She'd said nothing of Mother either increasing or decreasing the portions she delivered, so in that respect, Mother was consistent – but now that I was down here too, would that remain the case or would she make us split one sandwich? Share one cup of water? She was punishing us both but how far she'd go, I couldn't guess. A tidal wave of uselessness washed over me. It was simply impossible to work out what she would do.

My hand tickled. I flinched violently and squealed, brushing frantically at the place where traces of spider legs lingered tickling hideously. My skin crawled. I shivered again and hugged my knees, rocking back and forth on the bed and telling myself to calm down. Unheeding, my eyes streamed. Tears leaked down my cheeks and I tasted salt. The taste brought back a sudden memory of crying over the loss of my imaginary friend, Polly. I remembered curling up in bed, hugging myself, weeping quietly for fear *she* would hear me. Even then I had been fearful. At the age of six, just one year older than Emma, I had been frightened and uncertain of her reaction. She had always been unpredictable to me and she would always remain so, but there was a difference now.

I swiped my tears away and sniffed at my runny nose. Anger surged in my breast. There was an important difference now. When I was six, seven, eight, nine, ten, eleven, twelve I believed her to be some kind of perfect, all-knowing figure. Up until only a few months ago I had thought her almost Godlike, immortal, invincible. But now I knew better. She was human and she made mistakes. It was a simple truth I had long known about myself but I had never known it about her. Humans made mistakes and she was human. She was flesh and blood and bone. She could bleed too. She wasn't a saint; not even close to. She was damaged and that damage had turned her into an evil human being. Just because she was evil, didn't mean she was invincible.

My lips formed a tremulous smile in the unearthly darkness. Shakily, I pushed myself up from the bed. The mattress wheezed and I heard Sarah move. I listened to see if she was awake but her breathing resumed its steady rhythm, and I was struck by the calmness that her breaths reflected. In sleep and darkness, the emotions of the sleeping were hidden. I imagined what Sarah's face looked like now, so many years on from the horrific photograph of her tied to the bed when she was my age. I pictured the same widely spaced eyes and elfin nose grown larger, wrinkles lining the corners of her eyes. The vision was strangely vivid given it was an image conjured purely from memory and imagination. So too was the imagined frown etched between her brows like knife scores in ancient bark. I could not imagine suffering what Sarah suffered and being able to ever fully smooth the frown from my eyes.

Anger clenched my jaw and fists, and I strode forward blindly, snagging my tights on the scraggy brick wall. The material on my left leg tore. I winced at the faint screak of tearing elastic and wondered how far the ladder ran, fervently hoping it had not run all the way to my foot. My tights were another barrier between my bandaged feet and the grimy floor - not to mention the hundreds of spiders that haunted the place. Tights were my protection. My shield. My -

Tights. Tights? Tights...

Tights were pliable, strong, stretchy...tights could be useful...somehow.

The hint of an idea scratched at the back of my mind. Something to do with tights. Tights, tights, tights. I stretched and reached desperately for the idea, trying to pull the wafer-thin wisp into the centre of my mind and form it into something whole. I almost had it when Sarah gasped and the sound of metal scraping metal came from the door in the ceiling.

Chapter Thirty-Nine

"She's here," Sarah whispered. Her voice was high and hoarse, filled with a strange mixture of relief, fear and anger that chilled my blood.

"I'm going to try to reason with her," I whispered back, groping my way toward the stairs.

"Good luck with that," Sarah said darkly.

Another shiver prickled my spine. My hands found brick and I side-stepped as quickly as I could, heading in the direction of the steps. Above our heads the door opened a snatch and light winked and glimmered in the opening; one blinding ribbon of brilliant, shocking light that drew me like a bee to honey. Tripping over my feet, I stumbled, righted myself, side-stepped again. My foot found a step and I scrambled upward on my hands and feet.

The door opened several more inches flooding the first three steps with light, and I was abruptly possessed by an all-consuming need to bathe in that shimmering pool.

I glanced back into the gloom, which remained as ink-black as before. "Come up with me," I whispered urgently, "maybe she'll listen to you this time, if she won't listen to me."

"Fat chance," came her voice, which now sounded as hard as stone, the relief of before gone to dust. But her voice sounded closer and I wondered if she'd got off the bed.

"Please," I begged.

A hand holding a sandwich lowered itself through the opening. Food. My mouth began to salivate. I recognised those knuckles, that skin, those nails. It was her. Mother. Who else?

She placed the sandwich on the step, withdrew her hand then quickly lowered another sandwich onto the step beside it. Almost immediately I was overcome with relief: she was evil but not so evil that she would starve two helpless people to death. Hope spiked in my heart. She was not a lost cause. She would listen to one of us, let us reason with her, let us persuade her - and I had one glittering diamond with which to bargain. Something priceless she craved. The diamond was fake, but she wasn't to know that.

"Mother?" I said.

The hand was lowering a large plastic bowl of water through the gap now, and quivering from its weight. The hand stilled an inch from the step, quivering, responding to my voice.

She was human. She was only human.

"Mother?" I repeated. I reached out my hand and touched hers. Her skin was papery and hot. Her hand flinched at my touch and water splashed onto the step. I kept my hand on hers, my touch light.

"Mother? Please let me out. I miss you."

She placed the bowl on the step then withdrew her hand. I almost cried out for fear that she was going to lock us in again, but the door remained open. I raised my head and peered through. I could see her knees. She was kneeling on the ground on the roof of our prison. Behind her I could see the lushest of greens: grass. I could smell fresh air and grass and pollen and hear a bird tweeting merrily, unaware of the fear and misery happening at its feet.

"Mother?" I said, my heart was a throbbing lump in my constricted throat.

"I can't let you out," her voice was flat, void of emotion. Hard.

"Yes you can. You can let me out and we can be a family again. I will help with all of the chores around the house and we can keep each other company and dance to ABBA and -"

"No. That's simply not possible. Not now. Not now that..."

"That what?"

"That you know about *her*."

I knew she was talking about Sarah. I felt a hand on my back and nearly gasped. Sarah was on the step below me. Now that she was there I could feel her heat and smell her sweat. My own sweat was cold and ran in rivulets down my back. I looked at the sandwich, desperate to eat it but nauseous too.

"I won't tell anyone," I said, intentionally not saying Sarah's name. Last time I had said her name, Mother had gone ballistic.

"Oh I know that," she muttered, barking out a jagged laugh, "But you'll *know*, and I know you, Mirabelle. I know you won't be able to stop yourself from trying to let her out and that can never happen. She's evil personified. I've already told you that."

A saying I'd read in a book popped into my head. *Pot. Kettle. Black.* I'd not understood what it meant at the time, but sudden understanding flicked on like a light.

"Okay. I understand that, but you *can* let me out. I will be better, better-behaved, and I can help you find Clarabelle."

The diamond was out there now. It was my only bargaining tool.

If she didn't take it, I had no fall-back options.

I held my breath, and her breath hitched. Sarah's hand found my shoulder. It trembled. I could picture Mother frowning, thinking it through, her mouth a grim line, her small, dark eyes narrowed to slits.

"How?" she said slowly, drawing out the word.

This was it. The big lie. "She told me she was going to hide in the woods, near the cottage, next to this fallen tree we saw." I nearly added, *when we were running away from you.*

"Which fallen tree? There are hundreds of fallen trees in the woods."

"There was this huge one that I fell over. I can remember exactly where it is. I can take you there and we can bring Clarabelle home and start afresh and be a happy family, and I can learn how to make dresses and we can make dresses for Clarabelle and -"

"That's enough. Be quiet now. I need to think."

She let the door fall shut making me jump.

"Fucking psycho bitch," Sarah muttered, "she might actually be buying it."

"Here," I said, blindly feeling for a sandwich then turning round to hand it to her.

"Thanks."

I found the second sandwich and ate it like a wild beast, tearing chunks and chomping on them briefly before swallowing them down into my empty tummy. It was spam, but it was the best thing I'd ever tasted. When I finished the sandwich, I found the bowl and tipped water into my mouth, delighting, despite everything, in the deliciousness of the cold, crisp liquid. I was careful not to spill any. If Mother didn't let me out, we would need to make this water last a long time.

Carefully, I passed the bowl to Sarah and heard her drinking hungrily. She moaned with relief and burped. It would have been funny if not for the queasy uncertainty that plagued us. For a time that seemed impossibly long, we sat in silence listening, waiting and hoping she would open the door again, and that her answer would be the one we so desperately needed. I bit my nails and prayed to a god I didn't believe in. It was a simple yes or no answer. *Please say yes. Please say yes, please say yes. Please say -*

The door creaked open a few inches. Light shone in, golden and glorious. Birds sang.

"I've given it a long hard thought and I miss you too, Mirabelle. You'll never know just how much. Things have been hard, so hard. I've thought about letting you out hundreds of times. I nearly did once. I came out here and I stared at the shelter. I even pulled the key out of my pocket. I was so close to opening the door and letting you come back inside, but right at the last second I remembered how very badly you behaved, and I realised, as I've come to realise again, just now, that you are not the little girl you used to be. You used to be so pretty and kind and good. Such a good, beautiful, little doll, but you've changed. You've developed these strange, wild ideas about me and about yourself. You seem convinced I'm not your mother and it's hurt me very deeply. Too deeply. You've given me a wound that will never ever heal, but worse than that – if that's possible – is that I know you can no longer be trusted. I know you're lying to me about Clarabelle. I know-"

"No, Mother, please. Listen. I'm not lying about her! I promise you I'm not. I know where she is and I'll take you there. I'll-"

"Stop. You're embarrassing yourself now. My goodness Mirabelle, I've never heard you sound so pathetic. You're a nasty little liar. You're just as bad as her. You're both evil and evil deserves to be punished. Evil, evil, evil, evil little bitches!"

A scream-like roar tore itself from Sarah's throat, "YOU'RE THE EVIL ONE YOU FUCKING BITCH!"

She launched herself at the door like a bull on full charge. I slammed into the wall as she shoved past and watched in horror as, spitting murder, she got her head and arms through the gap and reached out wildly at Mother. Mother screamed and shoved Sarah's head back down into the shelter with a force that sent Sarah flying backwards, arms outstretched and flailing for the door opening. With a scream of rage, Mother slammed the door shut, trapping Sarah's right hand.

Sarah gave a blood-curdling scream, "My fingers! My fingers!"

"Oh no, oh no – what can I do?" I gasped.

Once again we were engulfed by darkness. I groped for her arm and trailed my fingers up toward her trapped hand. Mother was laughing manically on the other side of the door. She was trying to lock it, twisting the key in the lock and laughing but Sarah's fingers were stopping the door from locking.

"It hurts!" Sarah wailed.

Still laughing, Mother opened the door an inch and Sarah whipped her hand out with a wretched groan. The door shut and metal scraped metal.

"Evil deserves punishment," Mother shouted through the door. She banged twice on the wood and crumbs of dirt fell in my eyes.

Sarah moaned, "My finger...is...hanging off," then she slumped onto my lap, unconscious.

I stared at the place where the light had come in, heart pounding at what felt like two hundred beats per minute. I ought to have been terrified but I wasn't. I was angry, yes. Frightened, a little. But my strongest feeling was excitement.

When the light had shone in it had revealed things inside the shelter that I did not know were here. Things I could use. A plan began to unravel in my mind like thread from a torn dress – or the ladder in a pair of ripped tights. The plan depended on a couple of things going my way, but if they did go my way, it might just work. It might save us.

Chapter Forty

The air was redolent with the sickly-sweet scent of Sarah's blood and her body was like a dead weight on my lap. I heaved her off me and moved her down the steps as gently as I could, one step at a time. I was glad she was unconscious but worried about how much pain she'd be in when she woke up. I didn't have a clue what we were going to do about her hand. The only way to tell what kind of damage had been done would be to touch her hand, which would be agony for her. Her words rang in my mind, *hanging off*. Could shutting your hand in a door make that happen? Had Sarah imagined that or was her finger really hanging off. There was nothing down here to clean and bandage her hand with. Nothing to kill the pain. She was going to be in hell when she woke up.

Sarah was light so I was able to lift her onto the bed. I covered her with the bed covers then perched on the edge of the bed and took off my tights. My letter to my parents dropped onto the floor and I hoped my parents would never need to read it.

I was unable to rid my head of the hideous sound of Mother's laugh. I still couldn't believe she'd laughed. She actually enjoyed the sound of her own sister's pain.

My jaw clenched. I tried to focus on that laughter and how only an evil person could laugh like that. Only an evil person could do all of the things she had done. She had hurt other people but she had also hurt me very badly and I would stop her from doing anyone any more harm.

I slipped my right hand into the sock part of my tights then wrapped the tights round my four fingers as many times and as tightly as I could. Easing myself off the bed so as not to rock the mattress and disturb Sarah, I shuffled my way back to the steps. Beneath my bandaged feet the ground was gritted with dirt and who knows what else but I didn't focus on that. I found the steps more quickly than before. I was getting to know my way around.

In my mind's eye I pictured the place I'd seen the nail. It had been in the wall on the left of the door in the ceiling. Buried deep in the brick but not in completely. I needed that nail. It had been a big, long one – the longest, thickest nail I'd ever seen – and covered in rust, but it would do the job. If I could get it out of the wall.

I climbed to the third from top step and felt the wall with my left hand. Rough brick, rough brick, rough brick...metal! Scooting my bottom closely to the wall, I grabbed the rusted nail with my tight-bandaged hand and begin to twist with all my might. Tears ripped through the outer layer of the tights quickly but despite my efforts, the nail did not turn. The layering was too thick. It was protecting my fingers but it was also preventing me from working out the nail. I unwrapped three of the layers and tried again. No luck. Unwrapped another three. Tried again. Yes, I could get a grip on the nail now, but even after only ten twists my fingertips were beginning to burn. I kept twisting and tried wobbling the nail from side to side. I twisted and twisted, wobbled and wobbled. It didn't budge. I kept going, gritting my teeth against the pain, knowing I had to keep trying. I felt wetness between my fingertips and the nail and knew my fingers were bleeding, but I couldn't stop. I kept at it until my fingertips throbbed and I felt like I was going to throw up. I was about to stop when I felt it turn. Only once, half the way round – a minuscule amount, but enough to make me carry on.

*

I was sipping water from the bowl when Sarah moaned. I didn't know whether to be happy or scared that she was conscious.

"Polly! Help me – my finger – oh God, my finger."

"Hold on. I'm coming."

I carried the bowl down the steps and made my way back to the bed.

"You have to find something. Something to tie it on," she said.

"Tie it on?"

Her breaths were fast and ragged. "My finger. It's hanging off."

"Which finger?" I said as calmly as I could.

"My index finger."

I couldn't use my tights. I needed them, plus they were covered in muck, sweat and blood which wouldn't be good, if Sarah was right and her finger was actually hanging off. I racked my brain. I was wearing knickers and a dress. Nothing else. Both were dirty now.

"What can I use?" I said.

"I don't know. Oh God. It hurts so much. I'm losing a lot of blood. We need to stop the bleeding."

"What are you wearing?" I said.

She moaned. "Oh no – I'm going to be sick!" And she was. I felt something wet splatter my leg. At least she's done it on the floor rather than on herself.

"Have you got a T-shirt on that I can tear up to make some kind of a bandage? I can use a little of our water to clean it."

"Yeah. But I can't move my hand. I can't. You'll have to use my flares. Pull them off."

"No – what are we talking about – I can use some of the sheet, can't I?"

She moaned her agreement. The pain seemed to be getting harder to bear.

Quickly, I knelt on the ground by the foot-end of the bed, picked up the bed sheet and tried to tear it. It wouldn't work. I put it between my teeth and tore a strip off. Then another.

Sarah was muttering words I couldn't make sense of, moaning all the while. I dipped the first strip in the water and gently felt for her arm. She groaned.

"I'm going to clean it now," I said.

"No, no, no, don't touch it! It's too painful," she was crying.

"I have to. Like you said. We have to at least bandage it."

She screamed when I took hold of her palm, which was caked with blood. I felt her thumb, which was fine. My fingertips drifted to the right and then I felt it: a wet, fleshy stump. There was no finger attached anymore, and I wondered uneasily where it was. I dabbed the stump with the sheet and she screamed again. Vomit rose in my throat. I tasted sick.

"Okay, okay. I won't clean it. I'm going to bandage it as quickly as I can. Squeeze the mattress with your other hand and scream as much as you need to."

I didn't know how tightly to wrap it round her hand so I veered on the side of caution and didn't wrap it too tightly. She moaned and moaned and writhed around on the bed. I touched the bandage and felt blood soaking through already.

"It needs more," I said. I tore several more sheets off the bed, trying not to think about how filthy they probably were, then wrapped and tied, wrapped and tied until I couldn't feel any more moisture soaking through.

"It's done," I said, close to tears and suddenly shattered.

She continued to moan. I helped her drink water from the bowl then told her to try to get some sleep. I don't know if she slept because I fell asleep on the floor not long after and dreamt about Mother painting my face with blood.

*

Sarah drifted in and out of consciousness as I worked on extracting the nail from the wall. I couldn't tell how much time had passed since Mother had left, but it felt like a very long time. I was plagued by hunger again, there was only an inch of water left in the bowl and the fingertips on my left hand were raw bloody nubs now too. But I kept at it with few breaks, alternating hands when one felt too sore to twist the rusted nail. Wobbling the nail seemed to help a lot and little by little I felt the thin metal rod edge out from its brick prison. That was one thing that kept me going. Another was the fact that Sarah's hand felt strangely hot. When I hovered my hand above hers, heat radiated off like heat from an oven ring. And it was beginning to smell. It was a putrid smell. Did that mean it was infected? Did it mean she was dying? I thought about her twin boys and her husband and how devastated they would be if she died and I twisted the nail harder. I thought about Emma and hoped she had found her parents – or at least someone kind who could help her find them. Lastly, I thought about Patrick who was probably dead. I had barely known him but he had been a good man and he'd tried to help us. Did he have people out in the world who were worried about him? Did he have a wife or children or a mother and father? If he did, they would be going through hell right now. They would not know what had happened to him, what Mother had done to him. They wouldn't know he was a hero. Mine and Emma's hero. If I ever did get out of here I would make it my mission to find Patrick's family and tell them how brave he'd been.

Sarah groaned so I rushed back to the bed.

"Water," she croaked.

I lifted the bowl to her mouth and helped her sip.

"Careful. There's not much left now," I murmured, but she seemed not to hear me. I tried to move the bowl away but she grabbed it with her unharmed hand and held it fast. I was surprised by her strength.

"I have to tell you something," she rasped, "Before I die."

"You're not going to die. She'll come back soon and -"

"She's not coming back," Sarah said.

"Yes she is. She always comes back. You told me she comes back with food and water. She came back before, she'll come back again."

"It's too late. And I need to confess something. Something I've been holding in for a long time. Something I'll never forgive myself for."

"Don't be silly. You need to rest. You need to sleep. Sleep now, okay?"

"No. Polly, you need to know...what I did."

I shushed her and took the empty bowl away, placing it on the floor beside the bed. I didn't want her getting worked up. I patted her leg gently then went back to work on the nail, checking that my tights were still firmly in position. When Mother came back, I would be close enough to grab the tights and execute my plan. I only hoped I could get the nail out before she returned.

Chapter Forty-One

My fingers screamed. I tore off more sheet and wrapped up my fingertips, glad for once that I couldn't see anything down here. If I could see what my fingers looked like, I might not have continued working on the nail. Now that I had the nail clutched in my sweaty palm, I wondered if it had all been worth the pain and effort. If Sarah was right and Mother never came back my fingers would probably get infected and I'd die too.

Sarah was convinced she was going to die. If I didn't get her out of here soon, I knew she'd die. The stink of rot emanated off her hand in putrid waves and her body pulsed with unnatural heat. She'd tried again to tell me something but I'd silenced her. She needed to conserve her energy. I did too.

I got in position on the fifth from top step and pulled the tights taut. I had tied the tights around the inner handle of the door – the handle I had seen when Mother had come. The handle I had known would be our saviour, if things went to plan.

My muscles cramped so I shifted position for the tenth time. I couldn't afford to move from the step. If Mother came back, I had to be here, ready. This was my only plan. There was no plan B. Plan A had to work or Sarah would die and I would be next. I could already feel the cuts on my bloodied fingertips and bitten wrist beginning to itch, burn and swell. Soon there would be pus and the rats would come.

I waited. Shifted position again. *She has to come soon. She has to.* Blackness tugged on my eyelids. I could not remember the last time I'd slept. I battled and battled against the urge to drift into delicious oblivion and I won, for a time...

*

"She's here!" Sarah's voice hit my brain like a hammer.

My eyes flew open.

Metal scraped metal. I pulled the tights taut just as Mother began to pull on the door in the ceiling. She was strong but I was in a better position and prepared. My arm muscles clenched and I held fast to the tights as she tried and tried, cursing audibly, to open the door. I waited one more second. She had to be using maximum effort for this to work. I bit my lip and prayed again to a God I did not believe in, then I let go of the tights. The door flew open and light burst into the blackness. Sarah gasped. I gasped and raced up the steps and out, out into the outside. Blinded, I raised the nail. Mother had fallen onto her back – just as I'd hoped. Sandwiches littered the ground. She was stunned and spluttering furious, incoherent things, but she was already trying to stand. I threw myself onto her with a shrill shriek that I didn't know I possessed, and straddled her ribs. Without hesitating, I stabbed the nail deep into her upper arm. She screamed and her eyes went wide with shock and pain. I pulled out the nail and tried to stab again but she roared and rolled over, sending me sprawling onto my side in the long grass.

She crawled away from me. I scrambled to my feet and chased her, nail raised. I jumped onto her back and wrapped my left arm around her throat. She seemed possessed by inhuman rage and tossed me off her back. I hit the ground like a rag doll and she turned and grabbed my wrists and straddled me.

"Stop," she panted.

I struggled against her, writhing and thrusting and kicking out my legs but she had me pinned. Still I thrashed and thrashed. I was possessed and I wasn't giving in. Her hands squeezed my wrists so painfully that I nearly dropped the nail. Somehow I clung on to it. Her stringy hair dripped into my face and she shook her head, her eyes glaring. Behind her I saw blue sky and sparkling sun – so much beauty. My lungs burned. I could not go back in the shelter. No. Never.

I stopped struggling and turned my face to the side, forcing my body to go limp. I made tears come and fake-cried, made my chest heave with desperate sobs. She loosened her grip on my wrists and I brought up my knees and smashed them into her stomach. She made an 'oomph' sound and rolled onto her side. I pushed myself to my feet and ran. My plan was to lead her away from the cottage into the woods to the spot I remembered from before.

She chased me, screaming gutturally, sounding like a demonic beast. She was a beast. A murderous, insane beast.

I glanced back and saw her wielding something that glinted in the sunlight. A knife. She always carried a knife. I still clutched my nail, now bloody with her blood, but a nail was nothing compared to a knife.

I was shaking, legs wobbling like jelly, heart rattling about in my chest like shattered glass but I made my arms pump, made my legs move. I had never run so fast. I was a wild bird flying through the trees. The thought gave me strength. I ran on, jumping and dodging, thorns tearing at my bare legs, the torn bandages on my feet trailing behind me like blanched entrails ripped from a fresh kill.

The canopy above blinked light and birds cried out in horror, branches rustling as they scattered in fear.

"MIRABELLE! STOP!"

I looked back. She was gaining on me. Catching up. Hair wild, eyes crazed. But I was nearly there. I didn't know how I remembered where it was but I did. I saw trees I recognised, clumps of moss, a herd of white fungi. And I knew. I knew I was close.

Then I saw Patrick slumped up against a tree, his chin on his chest, eyes closed. Blood pooled around him. Caked him. Was he dead? I stopped and stared, breaths ragged. Maggots swarmed around his injured side. Flies buzzed in and out of the wound in a frenzied dance. His face was grey, his body as still as a stone figurine. Dead. Patrick was dead. A sob caught in my throat.

"Mirabelle."

I whirled around. She stood a few yards away.

"Get back!" I screamed, waving my nail wildly.

I stumbled back, nearly fell, regained my balance. She stepped forward, knife raised. Her shoulder dripped blood, her white blouse turning redder with every passing second. We stared at each other.

"I don't want to kill you but you've left me no choice," she said. Her eyes remained on mine. Her chest heaved.

I inched backward. My heart began to slow and an ethereal calm spread over me. I smiled and said nothing, just edged backward. She followed and tilted her head to the side. Her eyes narrowed and she glared murder.

"Stop now. Listen to Mother."

I continued to shuffle back then I stopped, anger rushing through me. "You deserved what your grandfather did to you. You deserved to be shut in there after what you did to that cat."

She barked out a laugh and shook her head. "I thought I raised you to be brighter than this."

I frowned, confused. "What do you mean?"

Her eyes clouded and glazed over. She spoke slowly, as if recalling a long-buried memory, "He didn't just shut me in that one time. He did it many, many times. And I didn't kill that cat. She did."

I said nothing, too stunned to speak.

"*She* killed that cat. Made it look like I'd done it. So beautiful, so perfect in Grandfather's eyes, but evil, so, so, so evil. She got me expelled. And Grandfather was worried I wouldn't learn my lessons, that I was bad because of what she made him think I'd done, so he shut me down there every day, to teach me a lesson. Oh yes, every day. Every day for three years. And I learnt alright. And you'll learn to."

I shook my head, trying to process her words, and knowing from the dreadful flatness in her voice that she was telling the truth. What that man had done to both of them was monstrous. Too horrible to imagine. Impossible to imagine.

I recalled Sarah's story. Why had she lied to me about the cat? To make me angrier, stronger, less scared of Mother? Or was she still lying to herself, all these years later?

Mother was eyeing the nail in my hand. She took a small step forward.

"Just let me leave," I said, inching back, "I'm not your daughter. Let me go home to my real parents. If you ever loved me in any way, let me go home."

She rolled her eyes. Took another step.

"Don't," I said.

She stayed where she was and jabbed the knife at me, each jab punctuating a syllable. "I'm not perfect. What mother is? But you, Mirabelle - *you* were supposed to be perfect."

"I'm not Mirabelle. My name's Polly," I said stiffly.

She seemed not to hear me. She stabbed again. Only two yards away now. "But you ruined that. All my efforts to make you the perfect little doll and what do you do? Betray me. Sneak around behind my back. Make up foul, hurtful lies about me. Try to leave me. Convince Clarabelle of your lies, make her turn on me too."

"It's not lies," I said through gritted teeth, "It's the truth. You kidnapped me ten years ago then you took Emma. You know that's the truth."

"No! You lie. You're evil, just like her." Her eyes became glittering jewels of black hatred and she advanced quickly.

"Get back!" I screamed, but she kept coming, moving faster, holding the knife high so that it caught the light and twinkled.

"You have to be punished. You were never going to learn your lesson; I see that now."

She lunged forward with an unearthly scream that echoed round us. The knife came. Long, lethal. The knife she used to slice through raw meat.

I threw myself to the side, hit ground, saw momentum carry her forward then down, down, down into the place I remembered.

Her body thwacked hard earth and bones cracked. She gave a

bitter, twisted screech, an anguished groan.

I twisted onto my hands and knees and crawled to the edge of the hole. It was deeper than Mother was tall. Cube-like in shape, its steep, vertical walls formed out of dark, damp soil. She lay on her side on a bed of green and yellow leaves, her greasy hair snaking out around her head like Medusa's serpents. Both of her legs were bent at awkward angles. Her complexion had taken on a sallow cast but two hot spots of colour dotted her cheeks. The knife was embedded to the hilt in her stomach. Blood bloomed and spread steadily and insistently across her blouse like lava across snow. Blood puddled in the leaves and seeped into the soil. She looked like a broken, bleeding scarecrow. She stared up at me, eyes glistering, and raised one arm.

"Mirabelle, please help me. Please help Mother. Mother needs you. Mother loves you."

Tears filled my eyes. Tears of relief and sadness and anger.

I turned to go.

"Mirabelle! Don't you dare! Come back! Help me! Help Mother!"

I turned back and looked down at her crumpled body and dark, crazed eyes. More blood oozed from her stomach onto the fallen leaves turning them black.

I sighed. In a low, steady voice I said, "My name's not Mirabelle and you're not my Mother."

In the not-too-far distance, sirens sang, their song the most beautiful sound I had ever heard.

Chapter Forty-Two

It was the first sunset I'd ever seen. I sat in the police car and watched the sky through the open window. The sky was layered. At the top ran a light, brilliant blue layer. Beneath the blue ran a delicate shade of orange followed by the most deliciously magical shade of light pink. It looked like someone had taken three brush strokes to the canvass above and painted the sky in three separate sweeps of colour. It didn't look real. Sitting here in the police car on the dirt road outside the cottage looking up at the sky didn't feel real. Watching Emma run down the dirt road toward me didn't feel real either. She was dressed in a pink T-shirt and white shorts. She looked clean and healthy and happy. On either side of her, jogging with her, were a man and a woman whose eyes were red and glassy. The woman was the spitting image of Emma.

A police woman with curly brown hair and a gentle, round face opened the door and I got out of the car.

"Polly! I'm so happy to see you!" Emma cried, throwing her arms around my waist.

I tried to smile but couldn't. I wrapped my arms around her little, sweet-smelling body and hugged her back.

She pulled away and crinkled her nose up at me, "You smell really bad."

Her parents smiled apologetically at me and her mother stepped forward, her big blue eyes brimming with tears. "Thank you so much, Polly. Thank you for saving our little girl. Can I give you a hug?"

I nodded and she enveloped me in a warm, gentle embrace. She pulled back and looked into my eyes, "You are such a brave girl. Thank you."

I choked back tears and nodded again. Emma wanted to tell me all about her adventure after I'd told her to leave me at the knacker's yard, but her parents told her firmly that I needed to rest. Emma gave me a hug goodbye and asked if she could come and bring me a present when I was feeling better. I said she could and watched her leave, skipping and chatting away happily to her parents almost as if nothing had ever happened.

Sarah waved at me. She was being rolled past in an ambulance bed. I waved back and watched her family hovering alongside the paramedics as they got the bed up and into the ambulance, wondering if her husband knew what she'd done to that poor cat when she was little.

The ambulance drove away and Emma's car followed. Policemen rushed around the cottage like giant, frenzied ants. The police woman stood in front of me, trying to hide the next bed that rolled past, but I could see the black body bag anyway. I knew it was Patrick and remembered my promise to find Patrick's family and tell them what he'd done for me and Emma. Another ambulance approached and Patrick was rolled into the back of the huge vehicle and driven away.

"You okay?" the police woman asked, "Can I get you anything?"

"I'm kind of starving to be honest, so yes please."

She smiled. "I think I've got some crisps in the glove compartment. Hang on a second."

While she rifled inside the front of the police car, I turned my attention back to the sunset. It was beautiful and if a thing could be perfect, this sunset was.

"Here you are," the police woman said, handing me a packet of crisps.

"Thank you."

"I've just been told we need to leave the scene now, so would you mind getting back into the car, Polly?"

I did as she asked.

"Make sure you strap in."

A memory of Mother strapping me in when she'd driven me back to the cottage made me flinch. I focused on my crisps, on the strong, salt and vinegar crunch of every bite.

As the police woman started the engine, I heard a howl and swivelled in my seat to look out of the back window. Mother was being wheeled into view. She was strapped to the bed but she was thrashing wildly from side to side and screaming. I swivelled round to face the front and my eyes met the police woman's in the rear-view mirror.

"I'm sorry you saw that," she said.

"It's okay. I've seen worse," I said. And I had.

"Would you like the radio on?" she asked.

"Yes please."

She turned it on and for a moment I was seized by the terrifying idea that ABBA would come on, but it wasn't ABBA. The radio man introduced a song called 'Welcome Back' by John Sebastian. I liked it.

My mind tried to return to when Mother and I had danced so I stuck my head out of the window and looked at the fields and the sky and the wide, open space of the outside. Cool air rushed at my face, soothing my aching head. The police woman passed me back a can of something called Coke that I had never tasted before. I liked that too.

We drove through countryside, past fluffy sheep and sturdy cows and beautiful sleek brown horses. I saw a few rabbits and more fields and more trees and bushes and a stream and then I saw houses, and more houses and I realised we were in an actual village or town. The police woman said something but I didn't hear her. I looked down at my cleaned and bandaged hands and watched them shake. I was beginning to feel nervous and cold, so I wound up the window and let my head rest back against the padded headrest. Tiredness dragged me down and I fell into a heavy, dead sleep.

"We're here," the police officer said.

I opened my eyes and looked out of the car window at a big building called 'Bristol Royal Hospital For Sick Children'. I didn't like the name of the hospital. A shiver ran across my neck and I snuggled down into the blankets that the police woman had piled around me. I stared at the huge, ugly, brown building and tears swam in my eyes. I didn't want to go in there. I didn't want to be inside. I wanted to be in the outside. I wanted to be free.

The car engine cut out and the radio went dead, cutting a slow, sad-sounding song in half. The police woman told me to stay where I was and got out of the car. I closed my eyes and pulled the blankets up over my head. I wanted to stay where I was. Good luck to whoever was going to try to get me to go into that horrid building.

A few minutes later, I heard the door next to me click open.

"Polly? Polly, it's okay. There're some people here you need to meet," said the police woman, her voice thick as if she was trying not to cry.

I stayed hidden, safe in my blankets, taking strange comfort in my own self-inflicted darkness. The blankets were warm and soft and they smelt clean. I squeezed my eyes shut and shook my head. There was a moment of silence then I heard a woman's voice. A different voice.

"Polly? Baby? Is that really you?"

My heart somersaulted. I recognised something in that voice. My brain seemed to click awake at its sound. Slowly, I unpeeled the blankets from around my face and stared at the fair-haired woman standing next to the police officer. She inhaled sharply. Silent tears spilled down her pale cheeks.

"Polly!"

She held her arms out to me. Her arms were shaking. Her whole body was shaking. She smiled, chin trembling, her eyes exactly like mine. Behind her stood a man with light brown hair. He was crying too. He sank to his knees and stared at me, his eyes wide and shimmering with tears.

The police woman smiled and stepped back.

I tore off the blankets and threw myself into my mummy's arms. Her arms wrapped around me and she held me and rocked me. She whispered my name over and over again. Her voice was so soft, so full of love. Another pair of arms wrapped around me and I knew they belonged to my daddy.

Acknowledgements

Thank you to my dad for being such an awesome editor, my husband for suffering my moany days and giving me his honest opinion, the girls at Godolphin School for their super feedback and the rest of my loved ones for their constant support and encouragement.

Printed in Great Britain
by Amazon